SCROLLING SHADOWS

Sucked into the Dark Side of Instagramverse
AUTHOR DIANE SHAWE

New Delhi • London

BLUEROSE PUBLISHERS
U.K.

Copyright © Diane Shawe 2024

All rights reserved by author. No part of this publication may be reproduced, stored in a retrieval system or transmitted in any form or by any means, electronic, mechanical, photocopying, recording or otherwise, without the prior permission of the author. Although every precaution has been taken to verify the accuracy of the information contained herein, the publisher assumes no responsibility for any errors or omissions. No liability is assumed for damages that may result from the use of information contained within.

BlueRose Publishers takes no responsibility for any damages, losses, or liabilities that may arise from the use or misuse of the information, products, or services provided in this publication.

For permissions requests or inquiries regarding this publication, please contact:

BLUEROSE PUBLISHERS
www.BlueRoseONE.com
info@bluerosepublishers.com
+4407342408967

ISBN: 978-93-7018-158-8

Cover Layout: Diane Shawe
Typesetting: Tanya Raj Upadhyay

First Edition: December 2024

DEDICATION:

This book is dedicated to my incredible mother, a woman whose unwavering strength, determination, and compassion have inspired me every step of the way. From the depths of my heart, I offer this tribute to a remarkable soul whose love and guidance have shaped me into the person I am today.

To my dearest Mum,

This is my first thriller. You have been the beacon of light in my life, guiding me through both triumphs and challenges with grace and wisdom. Your tireless work ethic has been an inspiration to witness. I have watched you dedicate yourself wholeheartedly to your profession, constantly seeking knowledge and self-improvement. Your passion for learning has shown me the importance of continuous growth and education, and I am grateful for the valuable life lessons you have instilled in me.

Your generous spirit knows no bounds. Time and again, I have seen you selflessly extend a helping hand to those in need, whether it's through your charitable work in the community or simply being a listening ear for friends and family. Your kindness and empathy have taught me the significance of giving back and showing compassion to others.

You have been an exceptional role model to everyone who has had the privilege of crossing paths with you. Your integrity, honesty, and unwavering moral compass have set a high standard for us all. You lead by example, and your actions have spoken louder than any words ever could.

Throughout the years, you have been my rock, supporting me through every endeavour and encouraging me to pursue my dreams.

Your belief in me has given me the confidence to face life's challenges and embrace new opportunities. Your love has been a constant source of comfort, reassuring me that I am never alone, no matter the circumstances.

As I write these words, I am filled with profound gratitude for the countless sacrifices you have made to ensure my happiness and success. Your unconditional love has been a gift beyond measure, and I cherish the countless memories we have created together.

Even though dementia has ravished your brain, you still manage to chuckle and laugh with that cheeky grin which tells us your still in there somewhere.

This book is a tribute to you, Mum, for all that you are and all that you have done. Your unwavering love and support have been the foundation upon which I have built my life, and for that, I am eternally grateful. I decided to let my imagination run free!

With all my love,
Diane (Dee)

PREFACE:

Delves into the captivating yet perilous world of social media addiction through the eyes of Amy Richardson, a 17-year-old girl consumed by her obsession with Instagram. Follow Amy as she innocently opens her Instagram app, and with each swipe she encounters a series of increasingly disturbing stories that seem to ensnare her within it's grasp. Struggling to break free, she finds herself trapped within the twisted narratives, unable to distinguish reality from fiction as Amy races against time to decipher the cryptic messages hidden within the stories to escape the clutches of the Instagramverse portal.

TABLE OF CONTENTS:

CHAPTER 1: AMY AND THE ALLURING ABYSS OF INSTAGRAMVERSE 1

CHAPTER 2: INTO THE VORTEX: THE NEW MYSTERIOUS EXPERIENCE 8

CHAPTER 3: THE REVENGE PUZZLE 13

CHAPTER 4: THE BOY BAND ENIGMA 17

CHAPTER 5: BEYOND THE GLAMOUR: THE HIDDEN DANGERS OF INSTAGRAMVERSE 21

CHAPTER 6: ADDICTION AND ESCAPISM: THE STRUGGLE WITHIN 28

CHAPTER 7: THE INSTAGRAMVERSE LABYRINTH 33

CHAPTER 8: THE ALLURE OF VIRTUAL LOVE 39

CHAPTER 9: THE INSTAGRAMVERSE MIRAGE 43

CHAPTER 10: UNMASKING THE SHADOWS 49

CHAPTER 11: THE STERN CONVERSATION 55

CHAPTER 12: "THE TIME TRAVELER'S QUEST" 59

CHAPTER 13: "FRIENDS AND PARTIES: TIME FOR SOME FUN" 65

CHAPTER 14: "THE DREAMWEAVER'S ENCHANTMENT" 68

CHAPTER 15: "DOING INSTAGRAM WITH DAD" 73

CHAPTER 16: "THE MIRROR OF REFLECTION" 76

CHAPTER 17: "THE EMPATH'S EMBRACE" 84

CHAPTER 18: "THE PUZZLE MASTER'S CHALLENGE" 88

CHAPTER 19: "THE WHISPERS OF THE UNSEEN" 95

CHAPTER 20 "LIFE IN THE REAL WORLD" 102

CHAPTER 21: BREAKING FREE FROM THE SPELL 105

CHAPTER 22: AMY'S MOTHER WANTED TO LEARN MORE 112

CHAPTER 23: HIDDEN AGENDA 117

ABOUT THE AUTHOR: 126

CHAPTER 1:
AMY AND THE ALLURING ABYSS OF INSTAGRAMVERSE

Amy Richardson was a typical 17-year-old girl (almost 18) with an insatiable appetite for adventure and a burning desire for recognition. In the real world, she often felt overlooked, like just another face in the crowded hallways of her high school. But in the digital realm, Amy found solace and escape in the mesmerising world of Instagramverse.

From the moment she created her account, Amy was drawn to the platform like a moth to a flame. Instagramverse offered her a sanctuary where she could express herself freely through captivating images and clever captions. It became her canvas, a place to curate the perfect image of her life, even if it was just a fleeting glimpse of reality.

Amy's addiction to Instagramverse stemmed from the validation it brought her. Every like, comment, and follower were a tiny dose of validation that temporarily eased her feelings of insignificance. The more she delved into the world of hashtags and filters, the more she yearned to be noticed, to have her uniqueness acknowledged and celebrated by others.

In the virtual realm, she wasn't just Amy Richardson; she was "AmyAdventurer," "AmyDreamer," and "AmyGoesPlaces." The world on the other side of the screen seemed larger, more vibrant, and full of endless possibilities.

Each day, Amy would immerse herself in the alluring abyss of Instagramverse, scrolling through countless profiles, admiring picturesque landscapes, envying the glamorous lives of influencers, and even occasionally connecting with like-minded strangers from distant corners of the world.

She felt an inexplicable connection to the images she saw, as if each picture told a story she yearned to be a part of. Amy's heart would flutter with excitement whenever she uploaded a new post, hoping for the flood of likes and comments that would affirm her worth in the digital landscape.

But, as her addiction grew, so did her disconnection from reality. Amy would spend hours on her phone, neglecting her studies, hobbies, and the people around her. Her real-life friendships became shallow, and she began to perceive her worth solely through the lens of Instagramverse engagement.

Amy's parents noticed the change in their daughter and expressed their concern. They worried that she was losing herself in the virtual world and becoming detached from the

richness of real-life experiences. However, Amy brushed off their worries, assuring them that she was just exploring her interests and finding herself through Instagramverse.

One evening, as the clock struck midnight, Amy found herself engrossed in her phone, mindlessly swiping through her Instagramverse feed. Her fingers danced across the screen, tapping on hashtags, and scrolling through captivating images. As she was mindlessly scrolling through her feed, Amy felt a strange sensation. Her eyes grew dizzy, and it seemed as if the screen was pulling her in, she shrugged it off.

Little did she know that this ordinary night of virtual exploration would lead her to an extraordinary discovery.

Amy was completely under her quilt, the lighting shone bright via her mobile phone. With each swipe, the world around her seemed to shift and morph. The once familiar interface of Instagramverse transformed into an ethereal landscape, bathed in an eerie glow. At first, Amy dismissed it as a mere trick of her tired eyes, but the sensation persisted, drawing her deeper into the digital abyss.

Intrigued and slightly apprehensive, she followed the path laid out before her. Each tap of a hashtag opened a portal to a new realm, each with its own unique and haunting atmosphere. The hashtags now held an ominous power, like keys to unlock forbidden secrets. Unbeknownst to Amy, these seemingly innocuous tags acted as gateways to a sinister parallel dimension, where perception became reality, and truth became tangled with fiction.

As Amy traversed this alternate Instagramverse, she realised that each hashtag carried consequences. Whether it was #EnchantingGardens or #WhimsicalWoods, every choice shaped the very fabric of the world around her. Some hashtags led her to breathtaking landscapes, filled with awe-inspiring beauty and wonder. Others plunged her into ominous realms, where darkness lurked at every corner.

In the heart of this strange realm, she stumbled upon an enigmatic and haunting hashtag: #ThePortalBeyond. A shiver ran down her spine as she sensed its significance. Instinctively, she knew that this hashtag was a key, but a key to what?

With newfound determination, Amy sought guidance from a mysterious companion named Nexus. A spectral figure, Nexus appeared to her in times of great uncertainty, offering cryptic hints and guiding her through the treacherous landscape of the Instagramverse. Nexus revealed that the portal to the real world lay beyond the elusive hashtag, but deciphering its true meaning was the ultimate challenge.

Amys eyes became heavy, it was 2am and the thought had crossed her mind that she should get some sleep. Her eyes grew dizzy again, and it seemed as if the screen was pulling her in. She tried to pull back, but it was too late. In an instant, she was sucked into her mobile phone, finding herself immersed in a surreal and wondrous world.

The transition was jarring yet exhilarating. Amy felt a sense of liberation as she stood in the midst of the digital landscape that had been her sanctuary for so long. But little did she know that her adventures had only just begun, and danger was lurking in the shadows of Instagramverse.

As Amy stepped into the virtual photo, she found herself immersed in a vibrant world of pixels and colours. The image was a picturesque landscape, with rolling hills, a shimmering lake, and a breathtaking sunset. But something felt off - it was as if the pixels held a secret, waiting to be discovered.

With her keen now awakened eyes, Amy began her search for hidden clues within the pixels. She zoomed in, scanning every inch of the image, looking for any irregularities or patterns. As she examined the pixels closely, she noticed tiny fragments that seemed out of place, forming a subtle trail leading towards the horizon.

Following the trail, she realised that the seemingly random pixels were a series of encrypted codes. Each colour and pattern held a unique meaning, and she had to decipher their message to proceed. It was a puzzle unlike any she had encountered before, requiring a combination of artistry and logic to unravel.

With her heart pounding, Amy diligently rearranged the pixels, piecing them together like a mosaic. The codes slowly revealed themselves, forming a sentence: "Seek the crystal key in the realm of reflections."

The message left her intrigued and slightly confused, but she knew it was a vital clue. Amy's mind raced with possibilities, and she speculated that the "realm of reflections" referred to a place where she could find mirrors or reflective surfaces within the Instagramverse.

As she explored different profiles, she finally stumbled upon one with an abundance of mirror selfies. Could this be the realm she was looking for? There, amidst the reflective images, she discovered a post that seemed to hold a hidden key - a crystal key figuratively hidden within the reflections.

The post's caption read, "Reflecting on the journey ahead," and the influencer seemed to be staring directly at something behind the camera, as if hinting at the presence of the crystal key.

Amy's heart leaped with excitement. She had found the key! Now, she needed to figure out how to unlock its power. With a hunch, she tapped the mirror selfie three times, mimicking the three beats of a drum. Suddenly, the image rippled like water, and a crystal key materialized in front of her.

The key glowed with an ethereal light, and as Amy held it, a portal appeared before her. It was a portal that would lead her to the next step in the maze. With a deep breath, she stepped through, feeling the rush of energy surround her as she journeyed deeper into the Instagramverse.

The Pixelated Path had been challenging, but Amy's determination had paid off. As she moved forward, she realised that each puzzle was not only a test of her intelligence but also a reflection of her growth and resilience. The Instagramverse maze was teaching her to see beyond the surface, to uncover the hidden truths, and to trust her instincts.

With the crystal key in hand, in this dark and twisted realm she found herself transported back into her bed with her mobile phone slightly under her pillow.

Amy was puzzled with this new game; she had not seen it promoted anywhere and none of her friends had ever mentioned it.

She thought for a moment what she had just experienced and concluded that perception was power, and authenticity was her strongest weapon, however she couldn't shake the feeling that her presence was not entirely her own. Unbeknownst to her, there were powerful forces at play, a mysterious entity manipulating the pixels and narratives of Instagramverse for its own malevolent purpose.

Amid the allure and excitement, Amy would soon realize that her addiction had exposed her to an unforeseen peril. The virtual world she had come to love held secrets that could lead her to her greatest triumphs or her most devastating downfalls. Anyway, she decided it was time to get some sleep.

The following morning, Amy woke up with a mix of emotions swirling inside her. Confusion, awe, and a hint of fear mingled as she tried to make sense of her extraordinary experience with her mobile phone and that weird game. The vivid memories of navigating through hashtags and facing that weird image and puzzle felt both surreal and hauntingly real.

As she gazed at her phone, the device that had unknowingly served as her portal into the digital abyss, she couldn't shake the feeling of being drawn back into that enigmatic world. Part of her yearned to go back, to continue the adventure and uncover the secrets that lay within the hashtags. The allure of the unknown, the thrill of discovering new realms, and the desire to reclaim control over her own narrative tugged at her curiosity.

Beyond the danger and challenges, Amy sensed an undeniable power within the Instagramverse. In this virtual realm, she had the opportunity to confront her fears, to explore hidden facets of her own personality, and to gain insights into the intricacies of human emotions and perceptions. The hashtags had become more than mere digital markers; they had become gateways to self-discovery and transformation.

Moreover, Amy felt a sense of responsibility. She had witnessed firsthand the malevolent forces at play within the Instagramverse – preying on vulnerability and the hashtags that shaped reality. As she navigated through the maze of hashtags, she had glimpsed the impact they had on the people trapped within their allure.

Amy realised that she had become more than just a passive observer; she decided that now she was a digital warrior, standing against the shadows that manipulated the Instagramverse. The urge to return stemmed not only from her own curiosity but from a deep-rooted need to protect others from falling victim to the hashtag horror.

Despite the dangers she had faced, Amy understood that the Instagramverse held secrets and insights that could reshape her perspective on reality. It was a place where perception and authenticity intertwined, forcing her to confront her own vulnerabilities and find strength in the face of illusion.

As the morning light filtered through her window, Amy decided, that when she went back into the Instagramverse, she would be armed with newfound knowledge and a stronger resolve. Her journey had only just begun, and she was determined to reclaim the power of hashtags for good.

CHAPTER 2:
INTO THE VORTEX: THE NEW MYSTERIOUS EXPERIENCE

Amy nestled comfortably in her favourite cozy nook, a tucked-away corner of her bedroom, surrounded by soft cushions and dimmed fairy lights. A book rested in her hands, its pages transporting her to another world. She loved losing herself in the captivating stories, savouring every word as she turned each page.

The book she was reading was a thrilling mystery novel, and the suspense kept her hooked. The characters came to life in her imagination, and she felt a sense of camaraderie with the protagonist, navigating the twists and turns of the intricate plot.

As she read, the minutes slipped by unnoticed, time becoming a distant concept in the realm of her book. The physical world faded away, and Amy was fully immersed in the fictional universe, feeling a surge of excitement with each revelation.

However, as she read further, a faint vibration disrupted her reverie. Her mobile phone, lying beside her on the cushion, illuminated with a notification from Instagramverse. Amy hesitated for a moment, torn between the allure of the book and the temptation of the virtual realm.

Curiosity got the better of her, and she set the book aside for just a moment. Amy picked up her phone and unlocked it, revealing the familiar Instagramverse icon on her home screen. Her thumb hovered over the app, a wave of anticipation washing over her.

Her love for Instagramverse was undeniable. It was a place of exploration, inspiration, and connection with friends and followers from around the world. She could discover new ideas, beautiful photographs, and share glimpses of her life with others.

But as she scrolled through her feed, she couldn't help but notice the subtle changes in her emotional landscape. The vibrant colours of her friends' vacations sparked a hint of envy. The picture-perfect meals shared by influencers stirred a feeling of inadequacy in her. The smiling faces and laughter of her acquaintances seemed to emphasize the loneliness she sometimes felt.

The virtual world of Instagramverse was a double-edged sword. While it provided a gateway to inspiration and joy, it also had the power to evoke feelings of comparison, insecurity, and isolation. Amy found herself wrestling with these conflicting emotions, her mind oscillating between the captivating fiction of her book and the alluring but sometimes disheartening world of social media.

The gentle whisper of the protagonist's adventures beckoned her back to the book. Yet, the notifications on her phone kept pinging, inviting her to venture deeper into Instagramverse's enticing abyss. It was a constant tug-of-war between the tangible and the digital, the real and the virtual.

It was a seemingly ordinary afternoon in the small town of Oakridge, where Amy Richardson lived. The sun cast its warm rays across the town, and the distant laughter of children playing in the park filled the air. Amy, found herself sitting on her bed, now engrossed in her phone's glowing screen, scrolling through her Instagramverse feed.

As she flicked her thumb up the screen, the images of perfect lives and smiling faces blurred together, creating a surreal kaleidoscope before her eyes. Lost in the digital world, she hardly noticed the room around her. But then, something strange happened—her vision began to waver, and a feeling of dizziness overcame her.

Amy shook her head, hoping to dispel the sudden light-headedness. Yet, instead of clarity, the sensation intensified. Her heart pounded in her chest, and she felt as if an unseen force was pulling her into the phone. Panic gripped her, but she couldn't tear her gaze away from the mesmerising vortex that had replaced her feed.

In a swift and disorienting motion, Amy found herself hurtling through a tunnel of swirling colours and shapes. It was as if she was being transported through the very fabric of Instagramverse itself. The world around her seemed ethereal and dreamlike, and she feared she might be losing her mind.

She tried to pull back, but it was too late. In an instant, she was sucked into her mobile phone, finding herself immersed in a surreal and wondrous world.

The transition was jarring yet exhilarating. Amy felt a sense of liberation as she stood amid the digital landscape that had been her sanctuary for so long.

When the chaotic whirlwind finally subsided, Amy landed with a thud on the ground. She looked around, blinking in disbelief at her new surroundings. She had entered the digital realm, and it appeared to be a story posted by one of her bullies.

Amy found herself trapped within the bully's narrative, a vivid reimagining of her own experiences through their lens. In this virtual dimension, her every flaw and insecurity were magnified, causing her heart to ache with hurt and frustration. The bully had taken her life and twisted it into a nightmare—a cruel and relentless reminder of her real-life struggles.

Yet, something unexpected happened as Amy navigated this twisted tale. She discovered that she possessed a peculiar power in this surreal world—she could influence the narrative. The more she immersed herself in the story, the more she understood its mechanics. The virtual realm, it

seemed, responded to her emotions and thoughts.

With this newfound awareness, Amy realised that she had a unique opportunity: the chance to take revenge on her bullies.

As Amy grappled with her conflicting emotions, she noticed a faint glimmer of light in the distance—a puzzle, it seemed, that held the key to her escape. To return to her own reality, she had to unlock the mystery of the bully's story, piece together its hidden elements, and find the strength to break free.

The puzzle was no ordinary riddle. It challenged her to understand the motives and vulnerabilities of the bully, urging her to empathize with the very person who had caused her so much pain. With each clue she deciphered, Amy gained deeper insights into the complexities of human emotions and the power of forgiveness.

As she journeyed through the bully's tale, Amy's heart softened. She realised that revenge might bring fleeting satisfaction, but it wouldn't heal the wounds that had been inflicted upon her. Instead, she longed for a sense of closure that could only be achieved through understanding and, perhaps, reconciliation.

Amid the backdrop of the virtual world, Amy embarked on an emotional odyssey of self-discovery. She learned that true strength didn't come from revenge, but from the courage to rise above hatred and find empathy in the face of adversity.

Amy finally pieced together the last fragments of the puzzle, unlocking the path to her escape. But instead of seeking destructive revenge, she made a bold decision—to confront her bully not with hate, but with compassion and a desire for understanding.

As she broke free from the bully's story, the digital world dissolved around her, and Amy felt herself being pulled back into reality.

With her feet firmly planted back in her bedroom, Amy took a deep breath, her eyes shining with tenacity. The encounter within Instagramverse's virtual abyss had left an indelible mark on her soul. The journey had only just begun, and she realised that, within the depths of this digital realm, lay not only danger but also profound opportunities for growth and empowerment. She now had to decide what form her revenge was going to take.

CHAPTER 3:
THE REVENGE PUZZLE

Amy sat with her guitar in her lap, fingers gently strumming the strings as she practiced a new song, she had been eager to learn. The melody filled the air, resonating with her heart as she perfected the chords and notes. Each pluck of the strings was a step towards mastery, and she felt a sense of accomplishment with each improvement.

But as she took a moment to catch her breath, her gaze wandered towards her mobile phone resting nearby. Its screen glowed invitingly, beckoning her to enter the digital realm of Instagramverse. The allure was tempting, and she felt a pull towards the virtual world.

Yet, she reminded herself of the joy she found in playing the guitar. It was a form of self-expression, a way to pour her emotions into the music. With renewed determination, she set her phone aside, choosing to continue her musical journey.

Amy returned to her guitar, determined to conquer the challenging parts of the song. Her fingers moved with precision, guided by the passion in her heart. The melody flowed through her, transporting her to a place of pure concentration and creative bliss.

In that moment, she realised that the guitar offered her a different kind of connection—one that was personal and fulfilling. While Instagramverse connected her to the outside world, the guitar connected her to herself. It was a reminder of her individuality, her unique voice in the symphony of life.

As she strummed the last chord, a sense of accomplishment washed over her. She felt an intimate connection to her music, a connection she knew could not be replicated in the digital realm. Amy understood that both pursuits—the virtual and the musical—had their place in her life.

So, she picked up her phone, not with a sense of guilt, but with a newfound appreciation for the balance between the digital and the tangible. Instagramverse remained a space of inspiration and connection, but she was now mindful of the moments she chose to engage with it.

Amy found herself entangled in the twisted narrative of her bully's story, facing the opportunity to exact revenge on Geoff, the tall and self-absorbed antagonist who took pleasure in tormenting her. He gelled his hair every day into a perfect Elvis Presley type style. As she navigated through the digital world created by the bully's post, a mix of emotions swirled within her.

Fuelled by years of frustration and hurt caused by Geoff's constant taunts and ridicule, Amy initially couldn't help but consider revenge as a viable option. The thought of turning the tables and making him experience even a fraction of the pain he had inflicted upon her was incredibly tempting. She envisioned scenarios where she humiliated him, just as he had done to her.

However, as Amy ventured further into the virtual labyrinth, she realised that revenge would only perpetuate the cycle of negativity. She questioned if stooping to his level would truly bring her the closure and healing, she desired. Deep down, she knew that responding with hatred and anger wouldn't lead to a resolution but rather to a perpetuation of animosity.

The puzzle that confronted Amy wasn't merely a physical challenge; it was a test of her character and values. It demanded that she confront her own demons and rise above the desire for vengeance. It required her to acknowledge the anger within her heart and choose a different path—a path of compassion, understanding, and personal growth.

As she thought about the revenge strategy she had concocted, Amy hesitated. She realised that while making Geoff experience discomfort might momentarily gratify her, it wouldn't make her the better person. It wouldn't erase the pain she had endured, or the scars left on her self-esteem. In fact, it might create more negativity and resentment within herself.

With each step she took in the bully's virtual world, Amy's perspective shifted. She encountered moments of vulnerability in Geoff's character, instances where he seemed unsure of himself, and fragments of his backstory that hinted at his own struggles. This insight humanised him in her eyes, reminding her that people are often driven to cruelty because of their own insecurities.

As she immersed herself deeper into Geoff's story, Amy found empathy blooming within her. She saw beyond the façade of the bully, recognizing that his actions were born out of his own pain and the need to feel powerful. The realization was a turning point, transforming her initial thirst for revenge into a desire for understanding and even forgiveness.

Amy knew that she couldn't change Geoff, but she could choose how to respond to him. Revenge would perpetuate the hurt, but compassion had the power to break the cycle. She decided that instead of executing her revenge plan, she would try to talk to Geoff, to appeal to his humanity, and perhaps even inspire a change in his behaviour.

In an unexpected twist, Amy crafted a different strategy—one that didn't involve humiliation or harm. She set up a scenario where Geoff walked into a room, only to find a straw like wig, carefully gelled in a Worzel Gummage hair style standing as a symbol of breaking free from his self-imposed perfectionism and societal expectations.

When Geoff discovered the wig, his initial reaction was rage. But as Amy looked into his eyes, she could see the confusion and vulnerability. In that moment, she took a deep breath and spoke from her heart, sharing her own struggles and how his actions had affected her.

In a rare display of vulnerability, Geoff listened, genuinely hearing Amy's perspective for the first time. It was a moment of raw connection between them, breaking the barriers that had separated them for so long.

Although Amy didn't receive an immediate apology or change in Geoff's behaviour, she knew that she had planted a seed of understanding. The revenge puzzle had transformed into a puzzle of compassion, and Amy had found the strength within herself to choose a higher path.

As she made her way out of the bully's narrative, Amy felt a sense of relief and newfound confidence in her ability to confront her own demons and rise above hatred. The revenge she once craved had been replaced with a yearning for understanding and healing—not only for herself but for her bullies as well. Oh and the ability to have a laugh.

CHAPTER 4:
THE BOY BAND ENIGMA

Amy stood beside her parents in the kitchen, apron securely around her waist. Together, they prepared dinner, chopping vegetables, stirring pots, and filling the air with the delightful aroma of a home-cooked meal. It was a tradition they cherished, coming together as a family to share the joy of preparing food and spending quality time with each other.

As they worked side by side, laughter and conversation flowed effortlessly. Her father playfully teased her about her guitar practice earlier, while her mother shared stories of her own adventures during the day. Amy relished these moments, cherishing the simple yet profound connections she had with her parents.

But amidst the warmth of the kitchen and the joy of family bonding, her mobile phone on the counter silently lit up with notifications. The allure of Instagramverse's virtual realm beckoned her, momentarily distracting her from the present moment.

Yet, Amy knew the value of these moments in the kitchen. They were moments of togetherness, of laughter, and of love—a respite from the digital world. With a gentle reminder to herself, she resisted the temptation to pick up her phone, choosing to stay present with her parents.

They continued to cook, her mother showing her a family recipe passed down through generations. Amy's heart swelled with gratitude as she learned the secrets behind the dish, knowing that she was becoming part of a beautiful culinary tradition.

When the meal was finally ready, they gathered around the dining table, savouring the delicious food they had lovingly prepared together. The conversation flowed, filled with anecdotes, laughter, and genuine connection. The joy of the meal extended beyond the taste of the food—it was the warmth of the moments shared with her family that made it truly special.

As the evening drew to a close, Amy found herself once again drawn into the enchanting depths of Instagramverse's virtual realm. This time, she was transported into the heart of a massive concert arena, surrounded by the electrifying energy of her favourite boy band's performance. She couldn't believe her luck as she watched her idols sing and dance with incredible charisma and talent.

However, her awe quickly turned to dismay as she noticed how the members of the boy band treated their backstage helpers. The lead singer seemed to have a

challenging personality, barking orders, and displaying an air of entitlement. He was a stark contrast to the image of charm and kindness that the band projected to their adoring fans.

Intrigued by the contradictions between their public personas and their true behaviour, Amy realised that her journey within the virtual realm wasn't just about exploring exciting fantasies; it was also an opportunity to witness the reality behind the polished facade.

As the concert ended, the setting shifted, and Amy found herself in the boy band's changing room. She was invisible to them, a mere observer in their private world. The members continued their banter, seemingly oblivious to her presence.

The lead singer, whom the world idolized, revealed a different side of himself behind closed doors. He treated the helpers with disdain, ordering them around and rarely acknowledging their efforts. The contrast between his public image and private demeanour left Amy feeling conflicted. She had admired him and his talent for so long, but this revelation cast a shadow of doubt over her perception.

Before Amy could process her emotions further, she noticed an intricate puzzle displayed on the changing room's wall. It was a complex web of enigmatic symbols, seemingly impossible to decipher. She understood that solving this puzzle was her ticket back to reality.

As she began to contemplate the puzzle's meaning, she noticed that the lead singer was carrying a heavy burden. He seemed overwhelmed by the pressures of fame, the expectations of fans, and the need to maintain a certain image. Amy's empathy stirred within her again, making her ponder whether his difficult personality was a result of the immense pressure he faced.

The puzzle seemed to reflect the complexities of human nature and the multifaceted personalities of the boy band members. Each symbol represented a different aspect of their lives—their struggles, dreams, and fears.

Amy realised that understanding the lead singer's true self was the key to solving the puzzle. She needed to look beyond his arrogant exterior and explore the vulnerabilities he hid from the world. It was a challenge that mirrored her own journey towards empathy and self-discovery, but she knew she had to persist.

As Amy continued to observe and listen, she caught glimpses of the lead singer's vulnerability. Beneath the bravado, she saw a young man who longed for genuine connections and the freedom to express his true self. Fame had trapped him in a relentless cycle of performance, leaving little room for authenticity.

As she pieced together the puzzle, Amy found herself drawing on her own experiences of feeling overlooked and struggling to find her place in the world. She realised that she and the lead singer were not so different after all—they both yearned for acceptance and understanding. In a moment of revelation, the puzzle clicked into place, and the changing room began to fade away. The lead singer turned to her, as if sensing her presence for the first time, and a flash of recognition crossed his eyes. He smiled faintly, as if acknowledging the connection, they had shared in that ephemeral moment.

With the puzzle solved, Amy felt herself being pulled back to reality, leaving the virtual realm behind. She returned to her room, feeling a mix of emotions—the thrill of the adventure, the awe of being close to her idols, and the burden of knowing their hidden truths.

This encounter with the boy band had taught Amy a valuable lesson—that even the most glamorous personas could hide vulnerable hearts. She understood that the virtual world often presented a polished version of reality, and true understanding required looking beyond the surface.

As she closed her eyes that night, Amy knew that her journey through Instagramverse's virtual realm was far from over. The allure of adventure and discovery still beckoned, and she was eager to face the puzzles and challenges that lay ahead. But more importantly, she was determined to carry the lessons of empathy and compassion from the boy band enigma into the real world, forever changed by her experiences within the digital abyss.

CHAPTER 5:
BEYOND THE GLAMOUR: THE HIDDEN DANGERS OF INSTAGRAMVERSE

Stepping into the sunlit garden, Amy felt an instant connection to nature's beauty. The gentle breeze caressed her cheeks as she picked up the watering can, ready to tend to her beloved plants. The vibrant colours of the flowers brought a smile to her face, and she relished the peacefulness that enveloped her.

As she watered each plant with care, she felt a sense of responsibility and nurturing. Her plants were like friends, each with their unique needs and personalities. Tending to them was not just a chore but a labour of love, a connection to the natural world that brought her joy and tranquillity.

Her mobile phone buzzed with notifications, but she decided to leave it on the garden bench for now. She wanted to fully immerse herself in this moment, to cherish the simplicity and beauty of nature without the distractions of the digital realm.

With each sprinkle of water, she noticed how her plants responded, their leaves seeming to perk up in gratitude. Amy felt a deep sense of fulfilment, knowing that she was playing a part in nurturing life and bringing beauty to her surroundings.

As she moved from plant to plant, she noticed a ladybug resting on a leaf, and a delicate butterfly fluttering by. The garden seemed to come alive with the presence of these tiny creatures, and Amy marvelled at the interconnectedness of all living beings.

The scent of earth and blooming flowers filled the air, and she took a moment to close her eyes, savouring the sensory delight. The garden was a sanctuary, a place where she could escape from the digital noise and find solace in the embrace of nature.

After carefully tending to all her plants, Amy finally picked up her phone. She noticed the notifications from Instagramverse but decided to savour the moment a little longer. She found a cozy spot in the garden, set her phone aside, and sat down with a book, letting herself be transported to another world once again.

The garden had become her refuge, a place of renewal and rejuvenation. With her mobile phone set aside, she embraced the tranquillity and connectedness she felt with nature. Amy learned that the digital world had its place, but it couldn't replace the beauty and serenity that the real world offered.

In the garden, time seemed to slow down, and Amy found herself present in the moment, fully attuned to the sights, sounds, and scents around her. It was a reminder of the simplicity and wonder that life had to offer, a sanctuary from the constant buzz of technology. But avoiding her phone was not easy especially as she had access to the Instagramverse vortex. She reached for her phone on the bench and clicked her Instagramverse icon.

As Amy continued her virtual adventures within the captivating world of Instagramverse, she gradually began to see beyond the glossy façade and glittering allure. The platform that had once seemed like a magical escape now revealed its darker underbelly, where dangers lurked behind the digital screen.

Among the various hidden perils, cyberbullying was one of the most prevalent. Amy encountered numerous profiles that spread negativity, targeted individuals with hurtful comments, and used the anonymity of the internet to perpetrate their cruelty. Witnessing the impact of cyberbullying on its victims left Amy disheartened, and she felt compelled to use her experiences to raise awareness about the importance of kindness and empathy.

Privacy concerns were another pressing issue she faced. Amy discovered that, in the quest for validation and recognition, many users often overshared personal information, unknowingly putting themselves at risk. The virtual world could be a breeding ground for predators and identity thieves, taking advantage of vulnerable individuals who trusted the anonymity of the internet.

As she explored Instagramverse further, Amy stumbled upon a profile that particularly alarmed her. It was labelled as "Kardashian Fashion," seemingly dedicated to showcasing the latest trends, styles, and advice for young girls. The allure of the profile's glamorous image attracted a large following of impressionable teenagers.

However, her gut feeling told her something was off about this profile. Upon digging deeper, she discovered the unsettling truth—it was not run by a reputable fashion influencer or stylist, but rather an elderly man with sinister intentions. He was using the façade of fashion and beauty to lure in young girls and exploit their trust.

Amy couldn't stand idly by, knowing that this profile was putting vulnerable users at risk. She knew that exposing this individual would be a daunting task, as the internet allowed for anonymity and swift disappearance. But she also understood that she had to do whatever she could to protect others from falling into this predator's trap.

Gathering evidence, Amy documented the discrepancies between the profile's glamorous exterior and the true identity behind it. She captured screenshots of suspicious conversations and interactions, while also researching any reported incidents associated with the account.

Just then through the corner of her eye she noticed that this man spotted her. She knew the only way to get back was to unlock the next puzzle. She grew nervous and started to panic, she could not find the puzzle.

Amy closed her eyes and when she opened them, she found herself surrounded with emojis, each one more puzzling than the last. The emojis seemed to be arranged in a sequence, but their meaning eluded her. She knew that decoding this Emoji Cipher was crucial to finding her way back to reality.

With a determined look in her eyes, Amy started examining the emojis one by one. There were smiling faces, hearts, lightning bolts, and even a mysterious eye symbol. She began to make a mental note of their order, trying to find any pattern or connection between them.

As she pondered over the emojis, she recalled an old emoji puzzle game she had played as a child. Maybe the solution was like that game, she thought. She experimented with different combinations, but nothing seemed to work.

Feeling a bit overwhelmed, Amy took a deep breath and reminded herself to approach the puzzle with a clear mind. She scrolled through the comments on the post, hoping for a clue. Suddenly, she spotted a cryptic message from her guide Nexus that caught her attention. "Unlock the gateway with emotions in your heart," the message read.

Emotions in her heart? Amy considered what the emojis might represent in terms of emotions. Smiling faces could indicate happiness or joy, hearts symbolized love, and lightning bolts might signify excitement or surprise. The eye emoji could represent curiosity or awareness.

"

Realization dawned on her as she deciphered the true meaning behind the emojis. They were not just random symbols; they represented emotions that resonated with the influencer's post. Excitedly, she rearranged the emojis in the sequence that reflected the emotions she believed they conveyed.

With a tap of her finger, she submitted her answer. The screen flickered, and the emojis transformed into a sequence of numbers and letters. It was a code, a message meant to lead her out of the Instagramverse.

Following the clues provided by the cipher, she navigated to a new profile that had recently posted a series of mysterious stories. The stories contained snippets of a riddle, and Amy soon realised that she needed to assemble the pieces to form the complete message.

Carefully piecing together, the stories, she uncovered the final clue that held the key to her escape. "Look beyond the image, seek the exit in the reflection." The message hinted at an image on the profile that concealed the portal she sought.

Amy scoured the profile for the image that held the hidden exit. She noticed a post with an intricate pattern, but when she focused on the reflection, she saw something remarkable - a portal embedded within the pattern.

Excitement surged just as she was about to tap, she felt a heavy hand grab her shoulder, she let out a scream as she tapped the portal, and the world around her shimmered. The next moment, Amy found herself back in her room, standing before her mobile phone. She had successfully unlocked the Emoji Cipher and discovered the path back to reality.

Grateful for her wit and determination, Amy realised that the puzzles had taught her valuable lessons about perseverance and thinking outside the box. Each challenge had been an opportunity for growth and exploration, and she felt more confident and capable than ever before.

Amy had work to do, she was determined to bring this issue to light, but she knew that doing so required careful planning. She decided to collaborate with her school's counsellor and her parents to ensure her actions were legal and safe. Her school counsellor provided guidance on how to report such activities to the appropriate authorities and organisations that could handle cyber safety concerns.

She composed a well-researched and empathetic message, outlining the deception perpetrated by the profile and the potential risks it posed to young girls. Amy emphasized the need for awareness and vigilance when engaging with online platforms. She encouraged her followers and friends to spread the word and be cautious of similar profiles.

As she hit "Post," her heart raced with anticipation. Amy knew that this could expose her to potential backlash, but she felt a sense of responsibility to protect others and make a difference in the virtual world she had come to know so intimately.

In the days that followed, Amy received an outpouring of support from her followers, friends, and even strangers who had seen her message. Together, they reported the profile, sharing the truth behind its façade. The community's collective action garnered attention from online safety organisations and even the media.

Through her brave actions, Amy not only exposed the dangers of this particular profile but also sparked a broader conversation about the hidden threats of Instagramverse. She joined hands with other advocates to raise awareness about cyber safety, the importance of verifying online identities, and how to protect oneself in the digital realm.

Her efforts led to the elderly man's arrest, serving as a powerful reminder that actions have consequences, even within the virtual world. While she was proud of what she had accomplished, Amy knew that her journey to make Instagramverse a safer place was far from over.

Amy faced the unsettling realities of the platform, from cyberbullying to privacy breaches. Her encounter with the deceptive "Kardashian Fashion" profile became a turning point in her mission to protect others and raise awareness about the potential hazards of online spaces.

As she continued her adventures within Instagramverse's virtual abyss, Amy carried the weight of responsibility on her shoulders, knowing that the digital world could be both a place of wonder and a dangerous labyrinth. Her journey of empowerment, advocacy, and self-discovery had only just begun, as she realised that the allure of Instagramverse held far more complexities than she had ever imagined.

CHAPTER 6:
ADDICTION AND ESCAPISM: THE STRUGGLE WITHIN

Sitting at her desk, Amy opened her journal—a safe haven for her innermost thoughts and feelings. The pen glided smoothly across the pages, as she poured her heart onto the paper. Writing was her way of processing emotions and finding clarity in a chaotic world.

In her journal, she expressed her dreams, her fears, and the adventures she wished to embark upon. Each word was a piece of her soul, revealing vulnerabilities and aspirations she seldom shared with others. The act of writing was cathartic, like unburdening her heart to a trusted confidant.

The soft glow of her mobile phone beckoned from the corner of her desk, but she chose to ignore it for now. This was her sacred moment of self-discovery, a chance to confront her thoughts and delve into the depths of her being.

As the words flowed, her mind felt lighter, and her heart felt freer. She confronted her doubts, fears, and insecurities, giving them voice through her writing. But she also celebrated her triumphs, dreams, and aspirations, finding inspiration within her own thoughts.

It was a moment of vulnerability and strength, as she faced her own truth and embraced her imperfections. In her journal, she was free to be unapologetically herself, without the expectations and judgments of the digital world.

After pouring her heart out onto the pages, she closed her journal with a sense of contentment. She knew that her thoughts and feelings were safe within those pages, waiting to be revisited whenever she needed solace or clarity. Reluctantly, she picked up her mobile phone, knowing that the digital world awaited. But this time, she approached it with a newfound sense of self-awareness. She recognised the value of her own thoughts and feelings, and she vowed to protect her vulnerability from the noise and superficiality of social media.

Amy scrolled through her feed, seeing glimpses of others' lives and their carefully curated posts. But now, she approached it with a discerning eye, knowing that behind the filters and captions lay the complexity of human emotions, just like her own.

As she navigated the virtual realm, she realised that her journal had become her anchor, a reminder of her authenticity and inner strength.

With her journal as her compass, Amy embraced the digital world with a newfound sense of self-assurance. She had learned to cherish her vulnerability, knowing that within it lay her true power— the power to be authentically herself, both on the pages of her journal and in the vast expanse of the virtual world.

Amy felt different about entering the Instagramverse vortex now, she felt stronger. She reached for her phone, but she still found herself wrestling with a deep internal conflict. The allure of the digital world had ensnared her, making her phone a portal to thrilling adventures and possibilities.

However, the recent encounters with the platform's hidden dangers had left her fearful and apprehensive about the phone's mysterious powers.

The desire to explore and escape the confines of her everyday life warred with the fear of the unknown that lay within her phone. The real world had its own challenges, and Instagramverse provided an enticing escape from them. The virtual realm allowed her to be anyone she wanted to be, far removed from the insecurities, and struggles that plagued her daily life.

Amy knew she needed to share her experiences with someone, to find support and guidance amidst the bewildering journey she had embarked upon. But who could she trust? Would anyone believe her extraordinary encounters within the virtual realm? The thought of revealing her surreal experiences to her friends or family seemed implausible. After all, how could she explain that her phone had become a portal to another world?

Her heart weighed heavy with loneliness and vulnerability. She felt as if she were trapped between two dimensions—the tangible reality she longed to escape and the captivating, yet perilous, virtual realm that held her in its thrall.

Amy's mind raced with questions and doubts. What if she got trapped in her phone and couldn't return to reality? How would she find her way back? Would anyone be able to help her, or would she be forever lost in the digital abyss?

In her solitude, Amy pondered the true meaning of escapism. She realised that while Instagramverse offered a temporary respite from her struggles, it couldn't provide a lasting solution to her challenges in the real world. If anything, the allure of the virtual realm had only complicated her emotions, blurring the line between fantasy and reality.

As her anxiety grew, Amy understood that she couldn't face these challenges alone. She needed to confide in someone she could trust.

The thought of her parents knowing about her adventures was daunting, but she also knew they cared deeply for her well-being.

Summoning her courage, Amy decided to share her experiences with her parents. Sitting them down one evening, she took a deep breath and began recounting her remarkable journey through Instagramverse's virtual abyss. She explained how her phone had become a portal and how she had encountered both wondrous adventures and hidden dangers within.

At first, her parents were sceptical, thinking she had merely indulged in vivid dreams or fantasies. However, as Amy spoke with heartfelt sincerity, they saw the earnestness in her eyes. They realised that her experiences, whether rooted or not, were causing her genuine distress.

Rather than dismissing her encounters outright, her parents listened with empathy and concern. They recognised that something profound had transpired within their daughter's mind, and they chose to support her emotionally, regardless of the nature of her experiences.

Amy's parents encouraged her to strike a balance between her virtual adventures and the real world. They acknowledged her desire to escape but reminded her that true growth and healing came from confronting challenges head-on, not running from them. They suggested seeking professional help to better understand her feelings and thoughts, and to equip her with coping mechanisms.

As Amy reflected on their advice, she knew they were right. She realised that her journey through Instagramverse's virtual realm had been a wake-up call—a reflection of her own desire for validation, belonging, and purpose. She understood that while escaping into the digital world might bring temporary reprieve, true fulfilment came from embracing her authentic self and facing her fears.

With newfound determination, Amy committed to exploring the digital realm with caution, being mindful of the dangers it held. She sought therapy to process her emotions and develop healthy coping strategies. Her adventures on Instagramverse now became a journey of self-discovery, empowering her to navigate both the virtual and real worlds with greater resilience and wisdom.

CHAPTER 7:
THE INSTAGRAMVERSE LABYRINTH

Amy's desk was a canvas of organized chaos, with textbooks, notebooks, and stationery scattered across its surface. She took a deep breath, determined to transform the clutter into a productive space for studying. With a sense of purpose, she began arranging her books neatly, stacking them according to their subjects.

As she organized her desk, her mobile phone sat quietly nearby, waiting for her attention. But Amy was focused on the task at hand—preparing her study materials for college. She knew the importance of creating an environment conducive to learning, free from distractions.

With each item she placed in its designated spot, she felt a growing sense of accomplishment. There was a sense of clarity and order that accompanied the organized desk, as if the physical space was mirroring the tidiness of her mind.

However, the allure of her mobile phone persisted, with notifications blinking invitingly. She knew she could easily get lost in the virtual world of Instagramverse or be tempted by the latest updates from her friends. Yet, she made a conscious decision to stay committed to her task.

Once her desk was in order, Amy opened her textbooks, diving her studies with determination. The words on the pages absorbed her, and she immersed herself in the subject matter. The mobile phone remained untouched, as she sought to absorb knowledge and expand her horizons.

After an intense study session, she couldn't resist glancing at her phone. But this time, there was no urgency, no desperation to check for updates. Instead, she used it as a reward—a moment of relaxation and connection with the digital realm after her diligent efforts.

Amy's disciplined approach to organizing her desk and studying materials had paid off. She found that the clarity of her physical space translated into mental focus, allowing her to dive deeper into her studies without succumbing to digital distractions.

She embraced a new routine. She dedicated focused study periods, free from the intrusion of her mobile phone, allowing herself moments of connection with her digital life only after completing her tasks.

As she navigated the virtual world with intention and discipline, she appreciated the importance of creating boundaries between her real and digital worlds. Amy's organized desk had become a symbol of her commitment to her studies and her self-awareness in managing the pull of the digital age.

With each day, she found a balance between the tangible and the virtual, cherishing her moments of focused learning while still enjoying the connections offered by her mobile phone. In the quest for knowledge, Amy had discovered the power of discipline and the value of being present in both the real and digital spheres of her life.

So, she had just completed her task and could not resist going into Instagramverse if only for a moment.

Amy, she found herself lured into a mystifying labyrinth that seemed to have no end. The digital walls twisted and turned, mirroring the complexity of her emotions and the challenges she faced in the real world. Each corner of the virtual maze represented a different aspect of her life, including her fears, insecurities, and internal struggles.

At the entrance of the labyrinth, Amy hesitated, unsure if she had the strength to confront her innermost demons. The virtual world had become a place of both wonder and peril, and this challenge seemed to be the most daunting yet. Nevertheless, she knew that breaking free from the labyrinth was essential for her growth and understanding of herself.

With a deep breath, Amy took her first step into the labyrinth, embarking on a journey of self-discovery. The walls seemed to close in around her, mimicking the suffocating feeling of her own insecurities. Each twist and turn forced her to face her fears head-on, bringing to light the doubts and uncertainties that had held her back in the real world.

As she navigated through the labyrinth, Amy encountered echoes of her past, moments where she had allowed fear to dictate her choices. She confronted memories of missed opportunities, self-doubt, and the times she had silenced her voice for fear of rejection.

But the labyrinth was not only a place of darkness; it also revealed moments of strength and resilience in Amy's life. As she progressed, she encountered memories of her small victories, the times she had overcome obstacles, and the friendships she had formed through kindness and empathy.

With each step, Amy realised that the key to breaking free from the labyrinth lay within herself. She needed to confront her fears, embrace her insecurities, and take control of her own narrative. It was a battle against the negative voices that had haunted her, a war waged against the self-doubt that had threatened to overshadow her potential.

In one particularly challenging corner of the labyrinth, Amy faced a metaphorical mirror that reflected her deepest fears and insecurities. Her reflection looked back at her with haunting eyes, revealing the vulnerability she had kept hidden from the world.

But instead of shying away from her reflection, Amy chose to embrace it. She acknowledged her imperfections and accepted that they were part of what made her human. In that moment, the labyrinth seemed to shift, the walls widening to make way for a newfound sense of self-compassion.

As she continued her journey, Amy's resolve strengthened. The walls of the labyrinth no longer seemed impenetrable; they became steppingstones for her growth. She understood that breaking free from the digital confines of Instagramverse also meant liberating herself from the shackles of her own insecurities.

In the heart of the labyrinth, she discovered a powerful truth—

that she held the key to her own freedom. Amy realised that the challenges she faced in the virtual realm were reflections of the struggles she carried in her heart. She couldn't escape the labyrinth without first confronting her inner turmoil.

With each stride of self-acceptance and courage, the labyrinth's walls began to crumble. The darkness that had enveloped her faded away, revealing a glimmer of light at the end of the maze. It was a light that symbolized hope, growth, and the promise of a more resilient Amy.

Finally, she emerged from the labyrinth, her heart pounding with a newfound sense of empowerment. The journey had been arduous, but Amy had faced her fears head-on, embracing her vulnerabilities and taking control of her insecurities.

So now all she had to do was unlock the next puzzle to get back to her bedroom. Having successfully navigated through the treacherous maze of illusions, Amy now faced the final challenge to get home-

In big letters, The Puzzle of Perspectives flashed in front of her eyes. The Instagramverse presented her with two conflicting stories about the place she needed to visit to return to reality. Each story painted a vastly different picture, and she could feel the weight of her decision hanging in the balance.

Her heart pounded as she carefully analysed both perspectives. The first story portrayed the place as a paradise, a breathtaking oasis of beauty and tranquillity. The influencer described it as a haven of peace, a sanctuary away from the chaos of the digital realm.

In contrast, the second story depicted the same place as a desolate wasteland, a forsaken corner of the Instagramverse. The influencer shared tales of danger and despair, warning against anyone venturing there.

Amy knew that one of these perspectives held the truth, while the other was a deceiving illusion. Time was of the essence, and she had to rely on her intuition and keen judgment to make the right choice.

Taking a deep breath, she closed her eyes and let her instincts guide her. She visualized the place in her mind, trying to sense the truth beneath the conflicting narratives. Suddenly, a gut feeling emerged, urging her towards one of the perspectives.

With her decision made, she tapped the screen, selecting the perspective she believed to be genuine. The moment she made her choice, the image on her phone flickered, and a portal materialized before her eyes.

The portal glowed with a soft, ethereal light, confirming her intuition was correct. Her heart filled with relief and excitement, knowing she had finally unlocked the path to return to reality.

Without hesitation, Amy stepped through the portal, feeling a surge of energy envelop her. In an instant, she found herself back in her own room, the familiar surroundings bringing comfort and reassurance.

As she set her phone down, Amy reflected on her journey through the Instagramverse. The Puzzle of Perspectives had been her ultimate test, and she had triumphed. It had taught her the importance of seeing beyond appearances and trusting her instincts.

With a sense of pride and newfound wisdom, Amy knew that she had grown stronger and wiser throughout this extraordinary adventure. As she moved forward, she carried the lessons learned from the digital labyrinth with her, knowing that the power to discern truth from illusion would serve her well in both the virtual and real world.

As she returned to the digital world outside the labyrinth, Amy knew that her encounters within Instagramverse's virtual realm were far from over. But armed with the strength she had found within herself; she was ready to face whatever challenges lay ahead. She understood that the true adventure wasn't just within the digital landscape but in the journey of self-discovery and growth that spanned both worlds.

CHAPTER 8:
THE ALLURE OF VIRTUAL LOVE

Amy stood in the kitchen, her eyes fixed on the digital recipe she had found online. The photo of the mouthwatering dish had sparked her curiosity, and she was eager to try her hand at cooking something new and delicious.

With her mobile phone propped up on the kitchen counter, she carefully followed the instructions, measuring ingredients and chopping vegetables. The tantalizing aroma began to fill the air as the dish took shape. Cooking was like a form of art to her, a creative expression that brought joy to both her and those she shared it with.

As she stirred the simmering pot, her phone buzzed with a notification. The temptation to check it tugged at her, but she reminded herself to stay present in the moment. This was her time to experiment, to immerse herself in the joy of cooking.

With every step, she felt a sense of accomplishment and excitement. Her mobile phone had become a digital sous chef, guiding her through the recipe, offering tips and tricks for culinary success. But Amy knew that the true magic of cooking came from the hands-on experience, the ability to adjust flavours, and the freedom to make the dish uniquely her own.

Finally, the dish was ready, plated beautifully on the dining table. Her family eagerly gathered around, their anticipation mirroring her own. As they took their first bites, their expressions lit up with delight. Amy beamed with pride, knowing that her culinary adventure had paid off.

After the meal, her mobile phone lay forgotten on the counter. The joy of cooking had transported her to a place of creativity and fulfilment, a place where she felt a deep sense of accomplishment. The virtual world could wait, for this moment of connection with her family was far more precious.

With newfound confidence, Amy resolved to continue exploring new recipes and experimenting in the kitchen. Her mobile phone remained a valuable tool for culinary inspiration, but she understood the importance of staying present in the physical act of cooking.

Cooking had become more than just a means of sustenance—it was a way for Amy to express her creativity, connect with her loved ones, and savour the joy of the present moment. Amidst her adventures and self-discoveries, she stumbled upon a new yearning—an innocent desire for her first kiss. The virtual world seemed like the perfect place to fulfil this curiosity, where the boundaries between reality and fantasy blurred.

In this vast digital landscape, she encountered someone who appeared to be her dream partner. Their profile exuded charm, wit, and kindness—qualities that resonated deeply with Amy. Engaging in playful banter and exchanging heartfelt messages, she felt an inexplicable connection to this person.

They seemed to understand her in a way no one else did, and she couldn't help but feel that destiny had brought them together within the virtual realm. As their interactions progressed, the possibility of experiencing her first kiss with this mysterious individual became tantalizingly alluring.

But as the virtual love story blossomed, a voice of caution echoed in the back of Amy's mind. She knew that the internet could be a realm of deception and manipulation, where people hid behind masks and false identities. The danger of falling for someone who might not be who they claimed to be was very real.

Amy's heart battled with her instincts, torn between the potential for a magical connection and the fear of being deceived. She wondered whether the charm she saw in the virtual world could ever translate into a real-life romance. Could this person be genuine, or were they merely a creation of someone hiding behind a screen?

Her friends cautioned her, reminding her of the potential dangers of forming intimate connections with strangers online. They urged her to prioritize her safety and to approach the situation with scepticism. But the allure of virtual love, the excitement of a first kiss, and the intoxicating emotions she experienced made it hard to resist.

Amy decided to take a step back and evaluate the situation with a clearer mind. She researched the individual's profile, seeking any clues or inconsistencies that might hint at their true identity. She also turned to online resources to learn about the signs of internet deception and catfishing.

Through her investigations, she discovered some discrepancies in the person's profile—a lack of personal photos, limited connections to real-life acquaintances, and vague details about their background. These red flags raised her suspicions even further, urging her to proceed with caution.

Amy realised that the virtual realm offered a blend of possibilities and dangers. While it provided an avenue for connecting with people from all walks of life, it also exposed her to risks she couldn't ignore. She acknowledged the importance of protecting herself, both emotionally and physically, and to be vigilant in her online interactions.

With a heavy heart, she gently withdrew from the virtual romance, opting to prioritize her safety and the integrity of her emotions. While she couldn't deny the allure of the connection, she understood that true love and trust could only be built on authenticity and honesty.

Amy's encounter with virtual love became a valuable lesson—a reminder that not everything within Instagramverse's digital realm was as it seemed. She learned to be cautious of the allure that could cloud her judgment and to listen to the voice of reason within her heart.

As she continued her adventures within the virtual realm, Amy's perspective on love and relationships evolved. She realised that true connections transcended the boundaries of screens and avatars, requiring honesty, vulnerability, and genuine affection.

With each step forward, Amy grew wiser and more resilient. The allure of virtual love might have tempted her, but she had discovered the importance of guarding her heart and approaching the digital world with a discerning eye.

CHAPTER 9:
THE INSTAGRAMVERSE MIRAGE

Amy's pet dog, Max, wagged his tail eagerly as he bounded towards her, a ball clutched in his mouth. His eyes sparkled with excitement, and he couldn't wait to embark on their daily adventure together. Amy's heart swelled with affection as she crouched down to ruffle his fur and exchange joyful kisses.

With her mobile phone tucked away in her pocket, Amy leashed Max and headed out for their neighbourhood walk. The sun painted a golden hue on the streets, and the fresh air invigorated their spirits. They were a team, exploring the world one step at a time.

As they strolled through the familiar streets, Max's tail swayed like a metronome, and Amy couldn't help but smile at his infectious enthusiasm. They greeted neighbours along the way, connecting with the community in a way that only Max could achieve. He brought joy wherever he went, brightening the day for anyone lucky enough to cross his path.

During their playful romp, Amy noticed a flutter of leaves in the distance. Curiosity piqued, she followed Max's lead, and they discovered a hidden path, canopied by lush greenery. Their adventurous spirits soared, and they ventured down the winding trail, their laughter mingling with the rustle of leaves.

As they navigated their way through nature's embrace, Amy's mobile phone remained forgotten in her pocket. She felt an unspoken bond with Max, a connection that transcended the virtual world. He reminded her of the beauty in simplicity, the joy of living in the moment, and the unbreakable bond between a pet and their human companion.

With each step, the worries of the digital realm faded away, replaced by the serenity of nature and the unconditional love of her furry friend. The world outside her mobile phone was teeming with wonder and enchantment, and she was grateful for the opportunity to savour it alongside Max.

When they returned home, the sun began to set, casting a warm glow over the horizon. Amy's mobile phone lay untouched, and she felt no urgency to check it. The day had been filled with laughter, companionship, and a connection that couldn't be replicated in the digital realm.

In Max's eyes, Amy saw the reflection of the purest love, untainted by the complexities of the virtual world. She resolved to cherish these moments with him, to prioritize the joy of playful walks and heartfelt connections over the lure of the digital screen.

With Max by her side, Amy discovered that life's most precious moments were often found in the simplest of pleasures—the feel of his fur under her touch, the sound of his joyful barks, and the bond that formed between them on their neighbourhood adventures. As they curled up together, basking in the warmth of their shared experiences, Amy's mobile phone remained forgotten, a testament to the irreplaceable magic of the real world.

Amy's life on Instagramverse was a carefully crafted mirage—an illusion of a vibrant and exciting existence. She would take numerous photos, apply filters to make them visually appealing, and curate her feed to present an image of a girl with a captivating life, surrounded by friends and a whirlwind of activities. In the digital realm, she appeared to be living her best life, capturing the admiration and envy of her followers.

But behind the screen lay a different reality. The more time Amy spent within Instagramverse's captivating abyss, the more she felt disconnected from the real world. The hours she dedicated to scrolling, posting, and engaging in virtual conversations left little room for building meaningful relationships in her everyday life.

While the illusion she created on Instagramverse seemed to satisfy her desire for recognition and validation, it also isolated her from authentic connections. Her virtual persona thrived, but her real-world relationships withered.

Inside the virtual realm, Amy could peer into the screens of other users, including her followers and those she followed. Amidst the seemingly perfect images and captivating captions, she caught glimpses of loneliness, insecurity, and the yearning for connection. She realised that she was not alone in feeling trapped within the confines of the digital world.

Amidst the challenges of the Instagramverse, one person who stood out to her was Jerome, a charismatic and popular boy in her class. Jerome had an effortless charm that seemed to captivate everyone around him. Teachers praised his academic achievements, and his peers admired his confidence and outgoing personality. On Instagram, his profile was a dazzling display of success and happiness, with pictures of parties, adventures, and smiling faces.

But behind the façade of popularity and success, Amy saw Jerome's life at home was far from what it appeared on social media.

In reality, Jerome's home life was rife with turmoil. His father, once a promising professional, had succumbed to the dark grip of drug addiction. He worked for a global brand, but his addiction had left him unreliable and volatile. At home, he subjected Jerome to relentless verbal abuse, creating an atmosphere of fear and sadness. The constant pressure to maintain his image as the perfect student and popular guy weighed heavily on Jerome's shoulders, leaving him feeling trapped and unable to express his true emotions.

Amy was organizing a group project, she made sure she was paired with Jerome. As they worked together, she noticed his hands shaking slightly, a sign of the anxiety he was trying to suppress. Amy's empathetic nature urged her to break through the barriers Jerome had put up to protect his secret.

In a moment of vulnerability, Jerome opened up to Amy about his troubled home life. The weight of his secret lifted as he confided in someone for the first time. Amy listened attentively, offering him a compassionate ear without judgment. For the first time, Jerome felt understood, and a newfound sense of relief washed over him.

As their friendship deepened, Amy encouraged Jerome to seek support from a counsellor or a trusted adult. Despite his initial reluctance, Jerome eventually reached out for help, taking the first step towards healing, and breaking free from the burden he had carried for so long.

Their bond strengthened over time, and Amy became a source of comfort and encouragement for Jerome. She reminded him that it was okay to be vulnerable and that true strength came from facing his struggles, not from hiding them. Through their friendship, Jerome learned the power of authenticity and found the courage to share his story with others who were going through similar challenges.

As Amy navigated the mysteries of the Instagramverse, she realised that the connections she forged in the real world were just as important. Her friendship with Jerome reminded her of the impact she could have on others simply by being there for them and showing empathy.

In the midst of the Instagram maze and its puzzles, Amy discovered the profound influence of compassion and support in the lives of those around her. The experiences she had within and outside the digital realm reinforced the importance of seeking help, fostering genuine connections, and embracing vulnerability. As she continued her journey, Amy carried this newfound wisdom, knowing that even in the face of a mesmerising but treacherous Instagram maze, true strength and resilience could be found in the power of friendship and understanding.

The virtual realm had become a paradox—a place that offered the illusion of connection and friendship while fostering feelings of isolation and loneliness. Amy understood that the superficial interactions and likes on her photos couldn't replace the depth and authenticity of genuine human connections.

As she delved deeper into the virtual lives of others, she noticed a common thread—an insatiable desire for validation, often leading to the creation of personas that projected an idealized version of themselves. The façade was intended to shield them from judgment and criticism, but it also prevented them from forming true, meaningful connections.

These realizations weighed heavy on Amy's heart. She yearned for true friendship and the warmth of genuine human interaction. She knew that to break free from the Instagramverse mirage, she needed to step back from the digital abyss and re-evaluate her priorities.

Amy made a conscious decision to reduce her time on Instagramverse and focus on building real connections with the people around her. She began to reach out to her classmates, engaging in conversations that went beyond likes and comments. She joined clubs and activities that aligned with her interests, where she could meet like-minded individuals in person.

As she invested more in her real-world relationships, she felt a profound shift within herself. The emptiness she had felt in the virtual realm started to dissipate, replaced by a sense of fulfilment that came from meaningful connections and shared experiences.

She also took the opportunity to open up about her struggles with social media and its impact on her life. To her surprise, many of her friends and peers shared similar sentiments, expressing their own battles with the Instagramverse mirage. They, too, longed for authentic connections and the freedom to be their true selves.

Through her journey of self-discovery, Amy learned that vulnerability and authenticity were the building blocks of genuine friendship. As she embraced her imperfections and allowed others to see her true self, she found that real connections formed effortlessly.

With each passing day, Amy's presence on Instagramverse became less about curating a perfect image and more about sharing her authentic experiences with her followers. She used her platform to raise awareness about the illusion of social media and the importance of fostering real connections.

CHAPTER 10:
UNMASKING THE SHADOWS

Amy sat in a quiet corner of her room, her mobile phone placed on a nearby table, intentionally out of reach. With her eyes closed and her breathing steady, she embarked on a journey of self-discovery through meditation and mindfulness. The world outside her room seemed to fade away as she immersed herself in the present moment.

As she focused on her breath, Amy felt a wave of calm wash over her. The tensions of the day slowly dissolved, replaced by a sense of tranquillity. With each inhale and exhale, she felt more grounded, more connected to herself and the world around her.

Her mobile phone buzzed with notifications, but Amy remained undeterred. This was her time to cultivate inner peace and embrace the power of mindfulness. She knew that the digital realm could wait, for this moment of self-care was a priority.

As she delved deeper into her meditation, Amy noticed her thoughts drifting towards the events of the day—the highs and lows, the worries, and aspirations. But she gently guided her focus back to her breath, finding solace in the simplicity of the present moment.

With mindfulness, she observed her thoughts without judgment, acknowledging them for what they were—mere passing clouds in the vast sky of her mind. She let go of the need to control or suppress her thoughts, allowing herself to be fully present in the here and now.

As the minutes ticked by, Amy felt a sense of renewal and clarity. Her mobile phone lay untouched, but she knew that when she did eventually pick it up, she would do so with a greater sense of balance and self-awareness.

With her meditation practice complete, Amy opened her eyes, feeling a newfound sense of peace and contentment. The world beyond her room remained unchanged, but she approached it with a fresh perspective—one that valued mindfulness and presence above the constant noise of the digital age.

As she reached for her mobile phone, she did so with intention, knowing that she had the power to choose how she engaged with the virtual realm. Mindfulness had become her anchor, a reminder to stay present amidst the distractions of the digital world.

Amy made mindfulness a regular practice, dedicating moments throughout her day to be fully present and grounded. With her mobile phone as a tool for connection rather than distraction, she embraced the power of the present moment, finding solace in the stillness within herself and discovering that true relaxation could be found without the need for constant digital stimulation.

However, on this day Amy continued her journey through Instagramverse's virtual realm, she stumbled upon a dark and malevolent presence lurking in the shadows. These malevolent entities manipulated users' desires and emotions, preying on vulnerabilities, and exploiting their deepest fears. The virtual world, once a place of wonder and excitement, now seemed like a treacherous landscape, with danger lurking around every corner.

As Amy was engrossed in her virtual adventures, she found herself entangled in a high-stakes puzzle that felt far more real than anything she had encountered before. The puzzle seemed to hold the key to her escape from Instagramverse, but it also came with a grave warning—the wrong move could trap her inside the digital world forever.

As Amy found herself in the midst of the Digital Enigma, she was faced with a perplexing challenge that required her to manipulate pixels and images. The Instagramverse presented her with a fragmented picture, scattered and disjointed like pieces of a jigsaw puzzle. She knew that to unlock her exit, she must rearrange the pixels to form a cohesive picture that held the key.

Her heart raced as she focused on the task at hand. With trembling fingers, she began to drag and shift the pixels, trying different combinations to create a unified image. Each move brought her closer to solving the enigma, but time was of the essence, and the dark entity's grip on her ankles intensified with every passing moment.

Fear crept into Amy's heart, and she felt a sense of desperation. She yelled for her mum, hoping that her voice would somehow reach the real world and bring help. But she knew that she couldn't rely solely on external aid – she had to trust in her own abilities to overcome the challenge before her.

The puzzle challenged her to confront her deepest fears and insecurities head-on. It presented her with a reflection of herself—the good and the bad, the light and the darkness. It was a test of her character, a battle between the allure of the virtual realm and her innate desire to escape its clutches.

She yelled for her mom again, the only person who might be able to help her in the real world. Her mom heard her spiritually, ran into her room and picked up the phone, her voice laced with concern and confusion as she tried to understand the situation. Amy explained the predicament she was in, the malevolent entities that had taken control, and the high stakes puzzle she needed to solve.

Amy's mom, though worried and uncertain about the situation, knew she had to think fast. She quickly searched for solutions online, trying to find any information that might help her daughter. But the virtual world had its own rules and secrets, and the answers seemed elusive.

With time running out, Amy knew she had to rely on her wits and intuition to navigate the puzzle. She took a deep breath, clearing her mind of fear and doubt, and focused on the clues that had been presented to her.

As she examined the puzzle more closely, she noticed patterns and symbols that seemed to hold significance. The malevolent entities seemed to feed on her fear and uncertainty, making her task even more challenging. But Amy refused to succumb to their sinister intentions.

With each step forward, she felt her strength and resolve grow. She realised that the power these malevolent entities held over her was fuelled by her own insecurities and doubts. If she could find the courage to face her fears and embrace her authentic self, the grip of the virtual trap might weaken.

Drawing on the lessons she had learned in her previous adventures within the virtual realm,

Summoning all her focus and determination, Amy pushed back her fear and dove into the puzzle with renewed vigour. She analysed the colours, patterns, and shapes of the pixels, searching for clues that would guide her to the correct arrangement. Each move became more deliberate and calculated, as she pieced together the image bit by bit.

As she manipulated the pixels, a glimmer of understanding started to emerge. The fragmented pieces began to form a coherent picture, and she felt a surge of hope and confidence. With each correct placement, the puzzle began to reveal its true nature - a mesmerising artwork that held the secrets to her escape.

However, the dark entity sensed her progress and grew even more relentless in its attempt to trap her within the Instagramverse. It tugged at her ankles, trying to drag her back into the digital abyss. Amy's pulse quickened, and she could feel her time slipping away.

Determined not to be defeated, Amy mustered her strength and focused solely on the puzzle. She ignored the dark entity's malevolent grasp, knowing that her freedom lay within her grasp. As she placed the final pixel into its rightful position, the image completed, and a brilliant light burst forth from the screen.

The dark entity recoiled, unable to withstand the light's power. Amy took her chance and broke free, tearing herself away from its clutches just in time. With a deep breath of relief, she found herself standing back in her own room, safely returned to reality in a flash of light, Amy no longer inside her phone portal or the virtual realm. Her mom hugged her tightly, relieved to see her daughter safe and sound. Amy knew that she had faced the ultimate test within Instagramverse's alluring abyss, and she had emerged stronger and wiser.

The malevolent entities and their manipulative tactics had been unmasked, revealing their vulnerability and insignificance in the face of authenticity and courage. Amy understood that the virtual world was not just a place of wonder and danger but also a reflection of the human experience—a mirror of desires, insecurities, and the eternal search for connection.

As she looked at her mobile phone, she realised that she had successfully worked out the Digital Enigma. The cohesive picture she had created held the key to her escape all along. Amy's heart swelled with pride and satisfaction, knowing that she had relied on her wit, courage, and determination to overcome the darkest challenges of the Instagramverse.

With the Digital Enigma behind her, Amy now faced the next chapter of her extraordinary journey. She knew that more trials awaited, but she was armed with the knowledge that she could conquer any enigma, no matter how daunting. As she continued her adventure, she felt a newfound sense of empowerment and confidence, ready to face whatever the Instagramverse had in store for her.

As she gazed at her phone, now just a tool rather than a portal, she knew that her journey with Instagramverse was far from over. But she also knew that the true power lay within herself—the power to navigate the digital landscape with wisdom, discernment, and a commitment to authenticity.

CHAPTER 11:
THE STERN CONVERSATION

In her room, Amy pulled open her wardrobe, the sight of old clothes and memories waiting to be rediscovered. With her mobile phone set aside on her bed, she began the process of sorting through the garments one by one. Each piece held a story, a chapter of her life etched into fabric and seams.

As she held a worn-out sweater, memories flooded back—a winter spent with friends, laughter echoing in the frosty air. Yet, she knew it was time to part with these clothes, to give them new life in the hands of those who needed them most.

The act of donating was more than just decluttering; it was an opportunity to spread kindness and compassion. Amy envisioned how these clothes could bring warmth and comfort to someone else's life, turning her act of generosity into a gesture of love.

Her mobile phone buzzed with notifications, but she chose not to be swayed by its call. This was a moment of selflessness, a chance to connect with her community in a meaningful way. She knew the digital realm could wait, for the real world beckoned her with a purposeful mission.

As she sorted through the clothes, she noticed pieces that no longer fit, a gentle reminder of growth and change. The act of letting go became a symbol of her own evolution, of shedding old layers to make room for new possibilities.

With each pile of clothes, she felt a sense of fulfilment. It wasn't just about donating, but about making a difference, no matter how small. Amy realised that the power to impact lives was within her grasp, and she didn't need a mobile phone to connect her to the world around her.

After gathering the clothes in bags, she picked up her mobile phone, knowing it could be used as a tool for good. With a few taps, she researched local charities and found the one that resonated most with her. She decided to drop off the donations and felt a sense of purpose in taking action.

When the day came to deliver the clothes, Amy was greeted with gratitude and smiles from the charity's volunteers. It was a humbling experience, knowing that her small act of kindness had the power to brighten someone else's day.

Amy made it a habit to give back to her community regularly, using her mobile phone to find opportunities to volunteer and make a difference. Sorting through old clothes had become more than just decluttering—it had become a gateway to compassion and generosity.

As she held her mobile phone in her hand, she felt a renewed sense of responsibility. The digital world offered her a platform to connect with others, but it was the actions she took in the real world that truly made a difference. Amy learned that the power to change lives was not confined to a screen, but rather, it emanated from the genuine kindness she extended to those around her.

Amy's mum and dad were deeply concerned about their daughter's recent experiences inside Instagramverse's virtual realm. The dangerous encounters, malevolent entities, and high-stakes puzzles had taken a toll on her well-being. They could see that Amy's time spent on the platform had not only isolated her from real-life connections but had also affected her emotionally and mentally.

One evening, her parents sat her down for a stern chat. They expressed their worries, emphasizing the need for her to strike a balance between her virtual adventures and her real-life responsibilities and relationships. Amy's safety and happiness were their top priorities, and they wanted her to take a step back and reevaluate her priorities.

Understanding the severity of the situation, her parents gave her an ultimatum—to reduce her time on Instagramverse significantly and to seek professional help if needed or face the consequences of losing her access to the platform altogether. At first, Amy felt defensive, but she could sense the love and concern behind her parents' words.

Feeling torn, Amy retreated to her room, her mind a whirlwind of emotions. She had become so entangled in the allure of the virtual world that she hadn't realised how much it had affected her real-life connections and emotional well-being. The thought of losing Instagramverse felt like losing a piece of herself, but she also understood the need to break free from its grasp.

The ultimatum presented her with a pivotal moment—a moment of self-discovery and growth. She knew that she had some difficult decisions to make, decisions that would shape her future and redefine her relationship with the virtual realm.

Amy sought solace in her journal, a place where she had always poured her thoughts and emotions. As she wrote, she confronted her own vulnerabilities—the need for validation, the fear of missing out, and the allure of virtual escapism. She realised that her time on Instagramverse had served as a distraction from the challenges and uncertainties she faced in the real world.

But amidst the introspection, Amy also recognised her strengths—the resilience she had gained from her adventures within the virtual realm, the empathy she had cultivated for others, and the desire to build meaningful connections.

To fill the void left by her reduced virtual presence, Amy embraced new hobbies, joined clubs and activities, and spent more quality time with her family and friends. She rekindled her love for reading, writing, and spending time in nature. As she engaged in these activities, she felt a sense of fulfilment she had been missing in the virtual realm.

Seeking additional support, she also reached out to a therapist, allowing herself to open up about her experiences and emotions. The sessions helped her gain valuable insights into her patterns of behaviour and thought, empowering her to develop healthier coping mechanisms and a deeper understanding of her emotions.

As the days turned into weeks, Amy noticed positive changes in her life. She felt more present and connected in her real-life interactions, finding joy in the simple moments and authentic connections with others. While Instagramverse still held some allure, she had learned to use it mindfully and as a means of genuine self-expression rather than seeking validation.

Her journey of self-discovery had taught her that true happiness came from embracing her authentic self, accepting her imperfections, and finding fulfilment in real-life experiences and connections. The virtual world could offer excitement and adventure, but it could never replace the depth and authenticity of human connection.

CHAPTER 12:
"THE TIME TRAVELER'S QUEST"

Amy stood in front of her bookshelf, a treasure trove of stories and adventures waiting to be rediscovered. With her mobile phone placed face down on the nearby table, she began the task of reorganizing her book collection. The books were like old friends, each one holding a special place in her heart.

As she carefully took each book off the shelf, she felt a rush of nostalgia. Memories of late-night readings and the magic of fictional worlds flooded her mind. With each book she rearranged, she was transported to different times and places, reliving the emotions and experiences she had felt while reading them.

Her mobile phone chimed with notifications, but Amy ignored the distractions. This was her time to immerse herself in the tangible world of literature, to touch the spines of her beloved books, and to connect with the authors' words and imagination.

As she reorganized the books by genre and author, she noticed how her reading preferences had evolved over the years. The stack of well-worn fantasy novels reminded her of her love for magical realms, while the rows of thought-provoking non-fiction books spoke to her quest for knowledge and growth.

With each book back in its rightful place, Amy felt a sense of satisfaction. Her bookshelf was more than just a collection of titles—it was a reflection of her journey, a library of the experiences that had shaped her.

Her mobile phone beckoned, but she hesitated to pick it up. The digital realm had its allure, but right now, she was content in the company of her books. There was something comforting about the tangible weight of paper and ink, the smell of the pages, and the excitement of turning each one to uncover a new story.

Finally, Amy decided to indulge herself in the pleasure of reading. She chose a book from her newly organized shelf, ancient Egypt, and as she opened its pages, she felt the world around her fade away. The characters came to life, and the images enveloped her in its embrace.

For a while, the mobile phone was forgotten. In the world of words, time held no sway, and Amy relished the escape into literary realms. However, in just a flash she realised that she could visit ancient places via her Instagramverse link and without any hesitation and a click Amy found herself standing in the vast desert of ancient Egypt as she entered the Instagramverse portal for her next adventure. The world around her was unlike anything she had ever experienced. The majestic pyramids stood tall against the horizon, adorned with intricate hieroglyphics and vibrant colours that told stories of a rich and powerful civilization. The aroma of exotic spices filled the air, and the bustling marketplace echoed with the sounds of merchants and traders.

Mesmerized by the beauty and grandeur of the Pharaohs' era, Amy couldn't help but marvel at the culture and advancements of ancient Egypt. She encountered historical figures like Cleopatra, Tutankhamun, and Ramses, each offering her a glimpse into their unique roles in shaping the course of history.

As Amy continued her journey through time, she found herself amid a different era—the suffragette movement. She witnessed the brave women fighting passionately for their rights and equality. Amy was deeply moved by their determination and courage as they stood up against societal norms and patriarchal oppression.

In each era she visited, Amy became an observer of pivotal moments in history, careful not to interfere with the timeline. She understood the responsibility she carried to preserve the integrity of the past, as altering even the smallest details could have far-reaching consequences in the present.

Through her encounters with historical figures and experiences, Amy gained a profound appreciation for the impact of the past on the present. She realised that the struggles and triumphs of those who came before had shaped the world she lived in today. History wasn't just a collection of facts and dates; it was a living, breathing narrative that connected everyone across time.

As she moved through time, Amy also learned the importance of preserving historical truths. She witnessed how stories and accounts could be twisted or forgotten over the centuries, and she vowed to be a guardian of authenticity and truth. She shared her experiences on Instagramverse, not just as thrilling tales of time travel, but as an opportunity to educate and enlighten others about the significance of history and its impact on the world.

Along her journey, Amy faced challenges that tested her commitment to non-interference. She encountered instances where her heart urged her to help or change outcomes, but she resisted the temptation, understanding that history should unfold naturally.

In ancient Egypt, she witnessed a rivalry between two powerful factions that threatened to escalate into a violent conflict. Amy had to make a difficult decision—to intervene or let the events unfold. She chose to mediate subtly, encouraging peaceful dialogue between the parties, without altering the course of history drastically.

In the suffragette movement, she witnessed a pivotal rally where tensions between protesters and authorities ran high. Her instincts pushed her to stand in solidarity with the women, but she resisted and reminded herself of her mission to observe without altering.

Through her choices, Amy not only preserved historical truths but also learned the importance of making a positive impact in the present. She shared the stories of the historical figures she met, reminding her audience of the significance of these figures' contributions to society. She also drew parallels between historical struggles and contemporary issues, inspiring people to stand up for justice and equality in their own time.

As Amy's journey through time came to an end, she felt a deep sense of gratitude for the opportunity to experience history firsthand. She had gained a new perspective on the interconnectedness of past and present and understood that everyone's actions, no matter how small, could leave a lasting impact on the world. She was daydreaming and completely forgot that she was still in the virtual world.

She just remembered she promised to play with her little brother and needed to get back. She looked around for the puzzle she had to unlock and just the saw a spinning wheel.

As Amy stumbles upon a trail of cryptic symbols scattered across various profiles. Each symbol appears to hold a piece of the puzzle, but she knows she must collect and align them on a virtual cipher wheel to unveil the hidden message that will lead her back to reality.

With a sense of urgency, she begins scouring different profiles, taking note of the cryptic symbols, she encounters. Time is of the essence, as she's aware that her brother will come looking for her soon. She hurries, tapping and saving the symbols on her phone.

Once she has gathered all the symbols, Amy opens a hidden feature on the Instagram app that reveals the virtual cipher wheel. The wheel is filled with concentric circles, each representing a different layer of the cipher. She must align the symbols in the correct sequence to unlock the message.

Her heart pounds as she starts placing the symbols on the wheel, trying different combinations in her quest to crack the code. With only 10 minutes before her brother arrives, she must think fast and stay focused.

The symbols seem to dance before her eyes, and she feels the pressure mounting. She takes a deep breath, trying to calm her nerves. She reminds herself that she has conquered challenging puzzles before, and this is no different.

As she aligns the symbols, she notices patterns emerging. Some symbols seem to fit naturally together, while others clash and create chaos. With each adjustment, the cipher wheel responds, indicating whether she's on the right track.

Time flies, and with each passing minute, the tension grows. Amy's heart races as she makes her final adjustments. She feels a surge of hope when the last symbol clicks into place, and the cipher wheel glows with a brilliant light.

In an instant, the hidden message is revealed, a set of coordinates and a series of words. It's the key to her escape. With a rush of adrenaline, Amy memorizes the coordinates and quickly takes a screenshot of the message.

Just as she completes the task, she hears her brother's footsteps approaching her room. She acts casually, leaving her phone on the bed as if she hadn't been doing anything unusual.

"Hey, Amy, what's up?" her brother asks, walking into the room.

"Oh, just browsing through Instagram," she replies with a nonchalant smile.

Amy's heart races as she hopes her brother wouldn't notice anything amiss. She engages in a brief conversation, trying to remain calm and composed.

That was close she thought, just imagine if he had closed the app! Amy knows she had overcome another Instagram enigma. The satisfaction of solving the cipher wheel in 10 minutes made her, more determined than ever to face whatever challenges lie ahead in her extraordinary adventure. With newfound confidence and a sense of purpose, Amy knows she's ready to take on whatever the Instagramverse throws her way, one enigma at a time.

As she stepped back into her own time, she carried with her a renewed sense of purpose—to be a steward of historical truths, to inspire others to learn from the past, and to make a positive difference in the present. The Time Traveler's Quest had been a transformative journey, one that would stay with Amy for the rest of her life, influencing the way she navigated the captivating abyss of Instagramverse and the real world beyond.

CHAPTER 13:
"FRIENDS AND PARTIES: TIME FOR SOME FUN"

Amy's heart raced with excitement as her birthday approached. Little did she know that her parents were busy planning a surprise birthday party that would become an unforgettable celebration. The day finally arrived, and as the clock struck six in the evening, the doorbell rang, signalling the start of the festivities.

As the door swung open, Amy's face lit up with joy as she saw her college mates and her best friend Demaria standing there with beaming smiles and colourful gifts in their hands. The surprise was a success, and Amy felt overwhelmed by the love and warmth radiating from her friends. They had gathered to celebrate her special day, and she couldn't have asked for a better gift.

The living room quickly transformed into a lively party hub, decorated with twinkling lights and colourful balloons. Her parents had spared no effort in creating the perfect ambiance. Amy's gaze fell upon a beautifully adorned cake in the shape of a mobile phone, complete with the iconic Instagramverse logo and eighteen candles shimmering on top.

"Happy birthday, Amy!" they all cheered, and she blew out the candles with a wish in her heart. The room echoed with laughter and joy as they clapped and sang the birthday song. Her heart swelled with gratitude for the friends who had come together to make this day so special.

Throughout the evening, laughter filled the air as they played games, danced, and posed for countless photos. Each moment was carefully captured and immortalized in the form of silly and fun poses for her Instagramverse posts. From goofy faces to group shots, the camera shutter never seemed to stop.

The night was a whirlwind of happiness and camaraderie. Amy felt surrounded by love and the genuine warmth of friendship. As the clock struck midnight, Demaria handed her a beautifully wrapped gift with a knowing smile. Amy's eyes sparkled with curiosity and excitement as she unwrapped it. Inside was a journal with a quote embossed on the cover: "The journey of a thousand miles begins with a single step."

"I thought this would be perfect for your new adventures," Demaria said with a wink.

Touched by the thoughtful gesture, Amy hugged her friend tightly. It was a reminder of the exciting journey she had embarked on within the Instagramverse and the discoveries she had made about herself and the world around her.

As the night wound down, Amy stood in the quiet aftermath of the party, reflecting on the happiness she felt in the company of her friends. It was a stark contrast to the virtual world of Instagramverse, where moments were fleeting, and connections sometimes felt superficial.

In this real-life celebration, she realised the importance of genuine connections and the value of creating memories beyond the confines of social media. The friends surrounding her were not just pixels on a screen; they were flesh and blood, and their love and support meant everything.

As the final guests bid their farewells, Amy felt a sense of contentment wash over her. Her birthday celebration had been a beautiful reminder of the joy of living in the present moment and cherishing the people who filled her life with love and laughter.

In the days that followed, as she posted some of the photos from the party on her Instagramverse, she felt a new appreciation for the platform. Yes, it was a place to share highlights and snapshots of life, but it was also a reminder to treasure the authentic moments that unfolded beyond the screen.

Amy's birthday celebration had marked a turning point in her relationship with Instagramverse. She would continue her adventures in the digital realm, but now, she was determined to strike a balance between the virtual and the real. And in doing so, she would create a life filled with joy, meaningful connections, and unforgettable memories both on and off the Instagramverse feed.

CHAPTER 14:
"THE DREAMWEAVER'S ENCHANTMENT"

After reorganizing her bookshelf a few days ago and indulging in the joy of reading, Amy settled down with her mobile phone, eager to connect with her grandma on a video call who couldn't attend her birthday party. The familiar chime announced her grandma's incoming call, and Amy's heart warmed with excitement. The screen lit up, revealing her grandma's smiling face, wrinkles etched with a lifetime of love and wisdom.

They chatted and laughed, bridging the distance between them with technology's magic. Grandma shared stories of her youth, and Amy listened intently, hanging on every word. The video call became a window into her grandma's world, a precious opportunity to feel her presence despite the miles that separated them.

As the call ended, Amy felt a profound sense of gratitude for the chance to connect with her grandma. The digital realm

had gifted her with a moment of cherished family bonding, and she cherished it in her heart.

Curiosity tugged at her, and Amy's fingers brushed over her mobile phone screen, opening Instagramverse. The virtual world beckoned, a tapestry of stories, images, and connections waiting to be explored. But she was mindful of the time spent there, knowing that genuine connections were not confined to a screen.

As she scrolled through the app, she felt a shift in her perspective. The moments shared with her grandma had reminded her of the real-life connections that mattered most—the warmth of family, the joy of face-to-face interactions, and the power of meaningful conversations.

Amy found herself navigating Instagramverse with intention. She sought out stories of positivity, inspiration, and genuine connections. She followed accounts that brought joy to her life, choosing to engage in conversations that added value to her digital experience.

The mobile phone had its allure, but Amy now understood the importance of balance. She recognised that while the virtual world offered entertainment and connections, the real world held the essence of authentic living.

In this delicate balance, Amy found contentment—a harmony between the digital and the tangible, reminding her that the true essence of life resided in both worlds, each offering its unique wonders and treasures to explore.

Tired she decided to go to bed early but sleep just wouldn't come so she decided to visit her Instagramverse with the hope of finding something soothing to help her sleep.

As Amy entered the virtual realm of Instagramverse, she found herself in a surreal dreamscape bathed in ethereal colours and shimmering lights. A mysterious figure, known as the Dreamweaver, stood before her. With an aura of enigmatic power, the Dreamweaver possessed the ability to manipulate dreams, using them as a conduit to explore the deepest corners of people's minds.

Intrigued yet cautious, Amy approached the Dreamweaver, eager to understand the nature of this unique encounter. The Dreamweaver explained that within Instagramverse, dreams held a special significance—their power to influence and shape reality was unparalleled.

Amy was offered a glimpse into the dreams of Instagramverse users, each dream an intricate tapestry woven from the dreamer's emotions, fears, and desires. But the Dreamweaver had something special planned for Amy—a journey into her own subconscious.

Reluctant yet curious, Amy agreed to let the Dreamweaver guide her through the labyrinth of her mind. She was transported into a dreamscape of her own creation, a world born from her thoughts and emotions.

In this dream, she encountered a seemingly harmless Instagramverse influencer known for selling "mega lashes." The influencer's posts were filled with images of impossibly long lashes that promised to transform anyone's look. However, as Amy approached the influencer in the dream, she noticed something unsettling—the lashes had a life of their own.

Suddenly, the mega lashes began to grow uncontrollably, turning into menacing tendrils that lashed out at Amy. Fear gripped her as she realised that this dream was mirroring her insecurities. The long lashes represented the pressure she felt to conform to societal beauty standards, and they were attacking her, symbolizing the inner struggle she faced with self-acceptance.

As the lashes closed in on her, Amy knew she had to confront her fears head-on. The Dreamweaver's voice echoed in her mind, guiding her to embrace her true self and find strength in vulnerability.

Summoning all her courage, Amy faced the lashes, acknowledging her insecurities and the unrealistic expectations she had placed upon herself. She realised that she didn't need to conform to someone else's idea of beauty to feel worthy or accepted.

With a newfound sense of self-assurance, Amy extended her hand towards the lashes, and a surprising transformation occurred.

The lashes softened and shrank, no longer menacing but simply a part of her dreamscape. They became a representation of her uniqueness and individuality.

As Amy navigated through her dream, she encountered other facets of her subconscious—an array of dreams, hopes, and fears that were woven intricately together. Some dreams brought joy and wonder, while others unearthed suppressed anxieties. With each encounter, Amy learned to face her emotions with compassion and acceptance.

At last, she stood before a mirror within her dream—a symbolic representation of self-reflection. Looking into the mirror, she saw her true self, embracing every aspect of her being, both the light and the shadows.

Having confronted her subconscious and embraced her vulnerabilities, Amy broke free from the Dreamweaver's enchantment. She woke up from her dream within Instagramverse with a sense of clarity and self-assurance.

As she journeyed back to reality, Amy carried with her a valuable lesson—that the power of dreams went beyond mere imagination. Dreams reflected one's inner world, offering an opportunity for self-discovery and growth. The encounter with the Dreamweaver had enabled her to understand the importance of self-acceptance and the need to let go of societal pressures.

From that moment on, Amy approached her interactions on Instagramverse with newfound authenticity. She shared her dreams, aspirations, and challenges without fear of judgment, understanding that vulnerability was not a weakness but a source of strength.

The Dreamweaver's enchantment had been a transformative experience, one that had empowered Amy to confront her subconscious and embrace her true self. With this newfound wisdom, she continued her journey through the captivating abyss of Instagramverse, navigating the virtual realm with authenticity and self-assurance.

CHAPTER 15:
"DOING INSTAGRAM WITH DAD"

Amy's dad had always been a bit of a mystery when it came to social media. He didn't quite understand the fascination with Instagramverse and preferred to 19 the moment, cherishing real-life experiences and connections. He was a simple man with simple pleasures - his love for Elvis Presley, his family, and his job as a bus driver.

One day, as Amy scrolled through her Instagramverse feed, she felt a twinge of longing. She wanted to share a special moment with her dad on the platform, to capture their bond and create a memory they could cherish together. But how could she convince her dad to participate in an Instagramverse post? The answer came to her in the most unexpected way - a chance discovery at a charity shop.

In the corner of the shop, amidst various odds and ends, she spotted a pair of blue suede shoes. She couldn't believe her luck when she saw they were her dad's size 11 and her size 5, and the price tag read £5 for the pair. The idea struck her like a bolt of lightning - she could recreate a small reel with her dad, mimicking Elvis Presley's iconic performance of "Blue Suede Shoes."

Excitement bubbled inside her as she shared her idea with her dad. To her delight, he agreed, intrigued by the prospect of doing something fun with his daughter. The following weekend, they set up a mini dance studio in the backyard. Amy propped her phone on a makeshift tripod, ensuring it captured the perfect angle.

With Elvis Presley's timeless hit playing in the background, Amy and her dad put on their blue suede shoes. They began to dance, playfully mimicking the legendary singer's moves with their own twist. Amy swayed her hips and shuffled her feet, trying to emulate the King of Rock 'n' Roll, while her dad added his signature flair and charm.

The joy that radiated from her dad's eyes as they danced together was priceless. In that moment, Amy saw a side of her dad she hadn't seen before - the carefree spirit of a man who was enjoying the simple pleasure of dancing with his daughter.

They laughed and stumbled through the dance, not taking themselves too seriously. Amy's heart swelled with love and appreciation for her dad, realizing that this was a moment she would treasure forever. The mobile phone recorded their goofy and heartfelt performance, capturing the essence of their connection.

After the dance was over, they sat together on the porch, catching their breath, and wiping away tears of laughter. Amy's dad admitted that he didn't quite understand the allure of Instagramverse, but he now understood its power to create and preserve cherished memories.

"I may not get this Instagramverse thing, but I get why it's important to you," he said, smiling warmly at his daughter. "It's a way to hold on to moments like this and share them with the world."

From that day on, Amy's dad didn't shy away from the occasional Instagramverse appearance. He became more open to capturing their moments together, whether it was enjoying a family meal, going on a spontaneous adventure, or simply sharing a laugh.

As they scrolled through the comments and reactions to their "Blue Suede Shoes" reel, they were touched by the heartfelt messages from friends and family who appreciated the genuine love and joy that radiated from the screen.

In that simple dance, Amy and her dad discovered the magic of Instagramverse beyond its digital realm. It was a way to connect with loved ones, create lasting memories, and cherish the precious moments that made life so beautiful. And as they continued to embrace Instagramverse together, Amy's dad felt a sense of inclusion, no longer left out of his daughter's world, but an integral part of it, dancing through life's ups and downs, one blue suede step at a time.

CHAPTER 16:
"THE MIRROR OF REFLECTION"

With her mobile phone lying face down on the dresser, Amy stood in front of the mirror, a smile playing on her lips. Today, she felt adventurous, ready to embark on a playful journey of self-expression through hairstyles. Her reflection stared back at her, a canvas for creativity and experimentation.

As she flipped through hairstyle inspiration on her phone earlier, she felt a surge of excitement at the endless possibilities. Now, with her mobile phone temporarily forgotten, Amy was fully present in the moment, ready to try out new looks and discover her own unique style.

With a hairbrush in hand, she began her makeover. She twisted her locks into intricate braids, her fingers moving with ease and precision. Each twist and turn revealed a different facet of her personality, an exploration of her versatility and individuality.

Amy's reflection beamed with satisfaction as she admired each new hairstyle. She tried high ponytails that exuded confidence, side-swept bangs that added a touch of allure, and messy buns that spoke of carefree charm.

Her mobile phone remained silent, but she knew she could document her journey later. This moment was about her, the pleasure of experimenting without distractions, and the joy of discovering new aspects of herself.

Next came the realm of curls and waves. Amy wielded a curling iron with finesse, transforming her straight locks into a cascade of bouncy curls. She ran her fingers through the curls, feeling the texture and marvelling at the transformation. Each hairstyle was a new chapter, a revelation of her evolving style and sense of self.

With her hair now a beautiful canvas of possibilities, Amy reached for hair accessories. Headbands, barrettes, and scrunchies—each one added a touch of flair to her creations. She adorned her hair with playfulness, allowing her creativity to guide her choices.

The mobile phone remained untouched, but Amy knew she would eventually share her hairstyle adventure with friends and followers. For now, this was a moment of self-discovery, an intimate exploration of her beauty and identity.

As she finally picked up her mobile phone, she was greeted by notifications and messages. Smiling, she clicked on the camera app, ready to capture her journey of hairstyles. The screen now reflected not just her reflection, but the essence of her spirit and the radiance of her joy.

Amy started to embraced hairstyling as more than just a grooming routine. It became an art form, a celebration of self-expression and personal growth. With her mobile phone by her side, she documented her hair journey, not just for validation, but to inspire others to explore their own creativity and beauty.

In the world of digital connections, the mirror and her mobile phone became allies in capturing her essence, allowing her to celebrate her unique beauty and embrace the journey of self-discovery with confidence and enthusiasm.

Forgetting she was on Instagramverse Amy's found that she took an unexpected turn as she stumbled upon a virtual mirror unlike any other. This mirror had the power to reveal alternate versions of herself in parallel universes, each representing different life choices and possibilities.

Intrigued yet cautious, Amy approached the mirror, unsure of what she would find. As she looked into its reflective surface, she saw a myriad of images—an array of different Amys, each living a unique life.

In one reflection, Amy saw herself as a successful entrepreneur, running her own business and achieving financial prosperity. In another, she witnessed a version of herself pursuing a career in the arts, fulfilling her passion for creativity and expression. Yet another reflection showed Amy as a globetrotter, exploring the world, and embracing a life of adventure.

With each reflection, Amy felt a mix of awe, curiosity, and uncertainty. She realised that each version of herself had made different choices, leading to vastly different paths in life. As she interacted with her mirror selves, she couldn't help but wonder which version of herself was the "right" one.

As Amy explored the reflections, she noticed something unsettling—the mirror's ability to present misinformation and fake news about her friends and loved ones. Doubt, jealousy, and gossip began to spread, affecting her perceptions of the people she cared about.

As Amy delved deeper into the reflections of the virtual mirror, she was taken aback by the unsettling scenes that unfolded before her eyes. The mirror seemed to possess an uncanny ability to tap into the darkest corners of her mind, presenting her with false narratives about her friends and loved ones.

In one reflection, Amy saw a fabricated story about her best friend, Sarah. The mirror projected an image of Sarah at a lavish party, surrounded by people Amy didn't recognize. Gossip whispered in her ear, painting a tale of betrayal and deceit, insinuating that Sarah was keeping secrets from her and had formed new friendships behind her back. Amy's heart sank as she watched the false portrayal of her friend. Doubt crept into her mind, and she began questioning the authenticity of her friendship with Sarah. She couldn't help but feel a twinge of jealousy and insecurity, wondering if she was truly important in Sarah's life.

Another reflection revealed a made-up story about her colleague, Jack. The mirror projected an image of Jack receiving a promotion at work, with a caption suggesting that he had achieved success through dishonest means, undermining his integrity and hard work.

The gossip in Amy's ear continued to plant seeds of doubt, leading her to question Jack's character and ethics. She found herself questioning her trust in him, wondering if he was truly deserving of his success or if there was a hidden side to his achievements.

As Amy explored more reflections, she realised that the mirror's ability to spread misinformation and fake news was causing a ripple effect on her perceptions of those around her. Doubt, jealousy, and gossip began to seep into her relationships, poisoning the trust and connection she had built with her friends and loved ones.

However, as the unsettling scenes unfolded, Amy knew she couldn't let these false narratives cloud her judgment. She remembered the lessons she had learned from her previous adventures, especially the importance of critical thinking and self-acceptance. She took a step back, reminding herself that the mirror's projections were not real. They were simply illusions created to test her inner strength and resilience. Amy understood that she needed to confront the mirror's deceptions head-on, refusing to let them taint her relationships and perceptions of the people she cared about.

With determination, Amy decided to challenge the mirror's illusions. As she touched the reflective surface, the distorted images shattered, revealing the truth behind the false narratives. In one reflection, Sarah was shown attending a family gathering, not a secretive party. In another, Jack was celebrating his promotion through hard work and dedication, not deceit.

With each illusion shattered, Amy felt a sense of relief wash over her. She understood that the virtual mirror's intention was to test her ability to discern truth from falsehood, and she had emerged victorious by embracing her critical thinking skills and trusting in her relationships.

She became aware of the power of misinformation on social media and how easily lies and rumours could spread, causing harm and sowing discord. The virtual mirror was a stark reminder of the need for critical thinking, discernment, and responsible sharing of information on platforms like Instagramverse.

Amidst the confusion and uncertainty, Amy realised that the mirror was not just a tool for self-reflection, but also a test of her self-acceptance and belief in her own path. It was tempting to compare herself to the different versions of herself and to others, to question her decisions and wonder if she had made the "right" choices.

But with each reflection, Amy understood that there was no single "right" path in life. Each version of herself represented a different facet of her desires, passions, and dreams. What mattered most was embracing her true self, acknowledging that her choices had led her to where she was in life—a place of growth, learning, and experience.

As the mirror continued to present fake news and misleading reflections, Amy realised that she had to stand firm in her values and beliefs. She knew that misinformation could harm not just individuals, but entire communities. She resolved to be a responsible user of social media, advocating for truth, empathy, and understanding in a world filled with misinformation.

It was time to get back to her room when suddenly, she is confronted with an overwhelming array of reflections, each one showing a different version of herself. She sees herself as fat, ugly, disabled, very thin, with a big birthmark on her face, and countless other variations. The reflections seem to taunt her, filling her mind with doubts and insecurities.

Feeling a surge of anxiety, Amy takes a step back, hoping to escape the maze of mirrors. But to her dismay, the reflections only multiply, creating an even more confusing and disorienting labyrinth. She realizes that she must confront this challenge head-on if she ever wants to find her way back to reality.

Drawing a deep breath, Amy gathers her courage and decides to tackle the puzzle. She takes a moment to examine each reflection closely, trying to discern the subtle differences between them. As she looks deeper, she begins to notice patterns and similarities among the reflections.

With each mirror she eliminates, the maze starts to shrink, but the task remains daunting. The reflections keep changing, showing her different aspects of herself. Amy feels a mixture of emotions, from self-doubt to acceptance, as she confronts the various versions of who she could be.

Suddenly, she remembers an important lesson she learned in her Instagram odyssey - the power of self-acceptance and embracing her true self. With newfound resolve, she stops trying to find the perfect reflection and starts looking for the one that resonates with her heart and soul.

As she continues to explore the maze, she notices that some reflections are superficial, merely capturing physical appearances, while others reveal deeper emotions and thoughts. She focuses on those reflections that reflect her genuine emotions and innermost feelings.

With each mirror she identifies as true to her essence, the maze shrinks further. Her heart beats faster as she gets closer to the exit, but she also realizes that the reflections reflect her inner thoughts and feelings, and accepting all aspects of herself is the key to escaping the maze.

After what feels like an eternity, Amy finally finds the one true mirror that accurately reflects her authentic self. As she gazes at her reflection, she feels a profound sense of self-acceptance and understanding. The mirror glows with a soft light, and a portal appears before her.

With a surge of relief and triumph, Amy steps through the portal, leaving the mirror maze behind. She finds herself back in her bedroom, standing in front of the same mirror when she was trying out new hairstyles.

As she looks at her reflection now, she sees herself in a whole new light. She understands that true beauty comes from within, and the reflections in the virtual mirror maze were mere illusions designed to challenge and test her.

Filled with newfound self-assurance and appreciation for her true self, Amy realizes that she has conquered the Mirror Maze. The experience has taught her the value of self-acceptance and the importance of recognizing her own worth, no matter how society or social media may try to define her.

With a smile on her face and a sense of empowerment in her heart, Amy is ready to face whatever lies ahead in her extraordinary journey through the Instagramverse. She knows that the path may be challenging, but she is equipped with the wisdom and resilience to navigate the enigmas that await her, one mirror at a time.

Through her journey with the virtual mirror, Amy learned the power of choice and the beauty of individual paths. Each decision she had made had shaped her into the person she was, and she embraced that wholeheartedly. She let go of the need to compare herself to others and to fictionalized versions of herself. Instead, she focused on being authentic, accepting herself and others for who they truly were.

CHAPTER 17:
"THE EMPATH'S EMBRACE"

With her mobile phone set aside, Amy sat engrossed in a documentary that had captivated her curiosity. The screen flickered with the raw reality of homelessness and its deep connection to mental health. Her heart ached as she witnessed the struggles of those marginalized by society, shedding light on a subject often overlooked.

As the documentary delved into personal stories, Amy found herself empathizing with the individuals on the screen. Their journey touched her deeply, stirring a desire within her to understand and make a difference.

The mobile phone sat silent; its usual allure diminished by the power of the documentary. Amy knew that this was a moment of learning and reflection, one that required her full attention and engagement.

As the stories unfolded, Amy found herself immersed in the lives of these resilient individuals. Their experiences were a mirror to the unseen struggles of so many, revealing the complexities of homelessness and mental health intertwined.

Her heart swelled with compassion and a longing to be part of the solution. This was more than just a documentary; it was a call to action; a reminder of the impact individuals could have on the lives of others.

After the documentary ended, Amy picked up her mobile phone with a newfound sense of purpose. She searched for local organisations dedicated to helping the homeless and supporting mental health initiatives. She wanted to be involved, to lend her voice and her efforts to bring about change.

With a few taps, she found opportunities to volunteer, to advocate, and to contribute. Her mobile phone had become a tool for connecting with meaningful causes, for bridging the gap between awareness and action.

Amy's mind was filled with thoughts and emotions as she scrolled through the information she had discovered. The digital realm now held significance beyond entertainment; it was a pathway to make a positive impact on the world.

In the days that followed, Amy immersed herself in volunteer work, dedicating time, and energy to supporting homeless individuals and mental health initiatives. She used her mobile phone to share stories of hope and progress, inspiring others to join the cause.

The documentary had become a catalyst for change in Amy's life. It had opened her eyes to the power of knowledge, empathy, and action. Her mobile phone was no longer just a portal to the virtual world; it had become a tool for creating real-world impact.

In this newfound balance, Amy found purpose and fulfilment. Her mobile phone became a reminder of the world's complexities, urging her to remain engaged, informed, and compassionate. With every documentary watched and every cause supported, she learned that the digital realm could be a platform for meaningful change, a force for good in a world that needed empathy and action.

As Amy delved deeper into the captivating abyss of Instagramverse, she found herself drawn into a unique digital realm where she gained empathic abilities beyond her imagination. Within this realm, she could feel the emotions of Instagramverse users and understand their struggles, connecting with them on a profound level. Amy came across a post from a user named Warren. His profile was filled with pictures of designer clothes, lavish vacations, and seemingly perfect moments. However, the caption beneath one of his recent posts hinted at a different story—one of loneliness and turmoil.

Curious and concerned, Amy reached out to Warren inside his Instagram post, offering a kind word of support. To her surprise, Warren responded openly, revealing the true struggles he faced behind the façade of his picture-perfect life. He confided in Amy that despite having all the material possessions, he felt unloved and neglected by his parents, who were always working and arguing.

Amy's empathic abilities allowed her to step into Warren's shoes, feeling the weight of his loneliness and desperation. She understood the pain he carried, seeking solace in the escape of late-night video games, a way to fill the void and distract himself from his emotional turmoil.

Determined to be a virtual guardian of empathy, Amy made it her mission to provide support and understanding to those in need on Instagramverse. She reached out to others who expressed feelings of sadness, anxiety, or isolation, offering a listening ear and a compassionate heart.

However, as she immersed herself in the emotional experiences of others, Amy realised the overwhelming nature of her empathic abilities. The barrage of emotions from various users threatened to consume her own emotional well-being. She struggled to find a balance between being a supportive listener and protecting her own emotions from being overwhelmed.

To maintain her equilibrium, Amy sought guidance from a wise Instagramverse mentor named Luna. Luna had experienced similar empathic challenges in the past and understood the importance of setting boundaries to preserve her own emotional stability.

Luna taught Amy how to create a safe space within herself, a sanctuary where she could process the emotions, she absorbed from others without being consumed by them. She learned to practice mindfulness and meditation; grounding techniques that helped her maintain a sense of self amidst the empathic storm.

Armed with Luna's wisdom and her own resilient spirit, Amy continued her role as a virtual guardian of empathy. She used her platform on Instagramverse to share messages of compassion, vulnerability, and understanding, encouraging others to open up about their struggles and seek support without fear of judgment.

As she interacted with individuals like Warren, Amy realised the profound impact that empathy and genuine connection could have on people's lives. Her empathic abilities allowed her to not only understand others but also offer meaningful support and encouragement, helping them feel less alone in their struggles.

Through her journey as the Empath Guardian, Amy learned the importance of self-care and emotional boundaries. She understood that while offering empathy and support was a beautiful gift, she needed to protect her own well-being to continue making a positive impact in the lives of others.

As she navigated the digital realm of Instagramverse with her newfound empathic abilities, Amy embraced her role as a virtual guardian of empathy and compassion. She vowed to use her platform to uplift others, creating a community where people could share their vulnerabilities and connect on a deeper level.

Her journey as the Empath Guardian was both a blessing and a challenge, but Amy knew that by staying true to her values and protecting her own emotions, she could be a source of light and healing in the captivating abyss of Instagramverse.

CHAPTER 18:
"THE PUZZLE MASTER'S CHALLENGE"

With a sense of creative excitement, Amy gathered her materials for a DIY project—a homemade candle-making endeavour. The table in her room transformed into a makeshift workshop, ready to be adorned with her handcrafted creations. Her mobile phone rested beside her, but she was determined to immerse herself in the hands-on experience before indulging in the digital realm. She melted fragrant wax in a double boiler, savouring the soothing aroma that filled the air. As she carefully poured the molten wax into containers, her artistic spirit flourished. Each candle became a canvas for her imagination, and she experimented with different colours and scents, eager to infuse her creations with personality and charm.

The process of making candles was meditative, a serene dance of creativity and concentration. The soft glow of the flame danced in her eyes, mirroring the spark of passion that drove her artistic journey. She was fully present in the moment, exploring the art of candle-making with joy and dedication.

Her mobile phone remained untouched, for the digital world held no allure compared to the tangible delight of her DIY project. This was her time to unwind, to revel in the joy of creation, and to connect with her artistic essence.

As the candles took shape, she admired her handiwork with pride. Each one held a unique beauty, an embodiment of her creativity. The mobile phone buzzed with notifications, but Amy was content to revel in her accomplishment, knowing she could always check later.

When the last candle had set, she admired the flickering flames, the gentle play of light and shadows. The ambiance was serene, a reflection of her inner calm and artistic fulfilment. The mobile phone was nearby, but it had become secondary to the moment of artistic bliss she had found. With her candles ready, Amy decided. She would gift them to her friends and family, sharing the joy of her DIY project with those she cared about. This was more than just a creative endeavour—it was a gesture of love and thoughtfulness, a tangible representation of the care she held for her loved ones.

Picking up her mobile phone, Amy smiled as she prepared to share her handmade candles on her social media. She felt a sense of accomplishment, knowing that she had made time for creativity and self-expression. Her DIY project had become more than just a craft—it had become a testament to the beauty of engaging in meaningful activities that brought fulfilment and joy.

Engaging in DIY projects and other creative pursuits became a regular part of her life, a reminder that the world beyond the mobile phone held a realm of fulfilment and self-discovery waiting to be explored. As she shared her creativity with others, she found that the digital world could amplify her joy and sense of connection, becoming a tool for sharing her artistic endeavours with the world. In this balance, Amy discovered that both the digital and the tangible realms had their place in her life, each enriching her journey with its unique and beautiful offerings.

When she decided to enter the virtual world, it was with purpose.

Amy started to venture deeper into the enigmatic depths of Instagramverse, she stumbled upon a series of mysterious puzzles that held the key to unlocking a powerful artifact. Each puzzle was a labyrinth of riddles, symbols, and cryptic clues, guarding a piece of the artifact that held unimaginable power.

One of the most intricate puzzles presented itself as a mesmerising mosaic, displayed as an Instagramverse post on an enigmatic user's profile. The mosaic featured an array of colourful tiles, each seemingly unrelated, but with a hidden connection waiting to be uncovered.

Amy's curiosity was piqued as she studied the puzzle. The cryptic caption accompanying the mosaic read, "In unity lies the key to untangle this enigma."

Feeling the weight of the puzzle's importance, Amy knew she had to unravel its secrets. As she analysed each tile, she noticed that several pieces formed patterns when arranged together. However, the tiles were scattered throughout different Instagramverse profiles, seemingly unconnected.

With the first clue in hand, Amy set out on a quest to find the tiles that belonged together. She spent hours navigating the intricate web of Instagramverse, connecting with users who unknowingly possessed a piece of the mosaic. Along the way, she made new friends, exchanged ideas, and discovered the beauty of collaboration within the digital realm.

As Amy collected the tiles, she began to understand the true essence of the puzzle's message—unity. Each tile represented a unique individual, but together, they formed something greater, just as a community on Instagramverse was more powerful when united.

With perseverance and the support of her newfound friends, Amy assembled the mosaic, revealing a hidden symbol that pointed her towards the next phase of the Puzzle master's challenge.

The next puzzle took her to the world of augmented reality, where she had to decipher clues scattered throughout various Instagramverse Stories. Each Story provided a glimpse into a different realm, and Amy had to immerse herself in the experiences to find the elusive clues.

The puzzles became increasingly complex and interconnected, testing Amy's intellect and intuition. With each solved puzzle, she gained new insights and abilities. She learned to think outside the box, to see beyond the surface, and to trust her instincts.

However, as Amy progressed, she sensed a dark presence watching her every move. A mysterious adversary had caught wind of the artifact's power and sought it for nefarious purposes. This adversary remained elusive, leaving cryptic messages and unsettling shadows across Instagramverse.

Amy knew she had to accelerate her efforts to protect the artifact from falling into the wrong hands. The puzzle master's challenge became a race against time, as the stakes grew higher with each puzzle she unlocked. As she approached the final puzzle, Amy felt the weight of responsibility on her shoulders. The artifact held immense power, and she understood that in the wrong hands, it could lead to chaos and destruction.

With determination and a newfound sense of purpose, Amy deciphered the last puzzle. The artifact's final piece revealed a hidden location—a virtual sanctuary within Instagramverse, a realm known only to those with pure intentions.

As she entered the sanctuary, she discovered the true nature of the artifact—it was not meant to be harnessed for power but to bring harmony and unity to the digital world of Instagramverse. It had the ability to amplify empathy, compassion, and understanding, connecting people in meaningful ways.

At that moment, the mysterious adversary revealed themselves— an individual consumed by greed and envy, seeking the artifact's power for their selfish desires. Amy confronted the adversary, determined to protect the artifact and its potential to foster positivity on Instagramverse.

As Amy delved deeper into the Puzzle master's challenge, she couldn't shake the feeling that she was being watched, as if a shadow lurked just beyond her sight. Cryptic messages started appearing in her DMs, accompanied by ominous symbols and enigmatic phrases. The unsettling presence seemed to grow with each puzzle she solved, and it became clear that an adversary sought the artifact's power for nefarious purposes.

As she unravelled the mysteries of each puzzle, Amy couldn't help but wonder who this mysterious adversary was and what their intentions were. The cryptic messages left her with more questions than answers, and she knew she had to stay one step ahead of this dark presence.

The clues led her on a digital chase across Instagramverse, following a trail of breadcrumbs that took her to hidden corners of the virtual world. The adversary seemed to be one step ahead, always just out of reach. Amy's empathy and intuition guided her, but she felt an increasing sense of urgency to protect the artifact from falling into the wrong hands.

Along her journey, she encountered other Instagramverse users who had also felt the adversary's presence. Some had been targeted with misleading information, while others experienced cyberbullying or had their accounts hacked. The adversary seemed to thrive on sowing discord and spreading chaos, using misinformation as a weapon.

Amy realised that the true power of the artifact was not just its ability to foster empathy and unity but also to counteract the negative influence of the adversary. The artifact could be a force for good, dispelling lies and illuminating truth, fostering understanding and compassion in a world where darkness lurked in the shadows of social media.

As the Puzzle master's challenge drew to a climactic end, Amy's determination to protect the artifact intensified. She knew that the adversary was closing in, and the final puzzle held the key to preventing the artifact from falling into their hands. In the heart-stopping conclusion, Amy confronted the adversary face to face. Their identity was revealed to be someone she had interacted with on Instagramverse before, someone who had disguised their true intentions behind a carefully crafted facade of positivity.

The adversary revealed their jealousy of Amy's growing influence and the power she held with the artifact. They believed that they deserved the artifact's power more and were willing to do whatever it took to claim it for themselves.

But as Amy faced the adversary, she understood that the true power of the artifact lay not in hoarding it for oneself but in sharing its transformative abilities with others. She tried to reason with the adversary, to show them the potential for positive change they could achieve together.

In a final confrontation, the adversary made a choice that would define their fate. Would they succumb to darkness and greed or embrace the power of empathy and unity?

In a moment of vulnerability, the adversary hesitated, torn between their darker desires and the chance for redemption. Amy reached out with empathy, understanding the turmoil within them, and extended a hand of friendship, offering a path towards the light.

In a surprising twist, the adversary chose redemption, realizing the destructive path they had been on. They confessed to their misdeeds and vowed to use their influence on Instagramverse for good, to make amends for the chaos they had caused.

As the adversary stepped away from darkness and towards the light, the unsettling shadows across Instagramverse began to dissipate. The digital realm felt lighter, filled with hope, and a sense of unity prevailed.

With the Puzzle master's challenge completed and the artifact secured, Amy emerged as a true guardian of empathy and compassion in the virtual world of Instagramverse. She knew that the battle against darkness was ongoing, but with the artifact's power and the support of her online community, she was ready to face any future challenges.

In the captivating abyss of Instagramverse, Amy's journey had taught her that true strength lay not in power or influence but in the connections, she fostered and the unity she inspired. As she continued her adventures, Amy vowed to use the artifact's power responsibly, to protect the platform from nefarious forces, and to shine a light on the potential for positive transformation within the digital realm.

As she continued her journey through the captivating abyss of Instagramverse, Amy carried with her the lessons and insights gained from the Puzzle master's challenge. She vowed to use the artifact's power responsibly, fostering a digital world filled with empathy, compassion, and unity—protecting the platform from darkness and guiding its users towards the light of positive transformation.

CHAPTER 19:
"THE WHISPERS OF THE UNSEEN"

With her mobile phone resting on the edge of the table, Amy found herself lost in the world of creativity, her sketchbook spread open before her. The blank pages beckoned, inviting her to give life to her imagination through art.

Her pencil danced across the paper, creating graceful strokes and intricate patterns. Each line was a glimpse into her soul, a reflection of her emotions, and a celebration of her unique perspective.

As she sketched, the world around her faded into the background, leaving only her and the artistic universe she had created. Her mobile phone remained untouched; its usual pull diminished by the allure of self-expression.

With each stroke of the pencil, Amy felt a sense of liberation and joy. The sketchbook was her sanctuary, a place where she could pour her heart and soul onto the paper without judgment or constraints.

She experimented with colours, blending shades and tones to bring her creations to life. Time seemed to lose its meaning as she immersed herself in the artistic flow, each stroke building upon the last.

The mobile phone buzzed with notifications, but she ignored the distractions. This was her time to create, to let her imagination run wild, and to find solace in the beauty of art.

As her sketches took shape, a story unfolded on the pages. Each drawing told a different tale—a whimsical landscape, a portrait of a loved one, a burst of abstract expressionism.

Amy's mobile phone sat idle, and she felt a sense of peace in its silence. In this moment of artistic exploration, the digital realm faded into insignificance.

When she finally put her pencil down, her sketchbook had become a testament to her creativity. The pages were filled with art that encapsulated her emotions, thoughts, and dreams. With a satisfied smile, she picked up her mobile phone. She knew that while the digital world held its allure, her sketchbook was a treasure trove of inspiration and self-discovery.

Her mobile phone remained a valuable tool for sharing her artwork and connecting with fellow artists, but she now understood the importance of embracing the tangible joy of creativity.

In the pages of her sketchbook, Amy found solace, expression, and a profound connection with her inner self. As she continued to create, she discovered that her art held the power to touch hearts, inspire others, and bring beauty into the world.

In this balance of the digital and the tangible, Amy noticed faint whispers and fleeting images of shadowy figures that seemed to dance at the edges of her vision inside Instagramverse. At first, she dismissed them as mere tricks of the imagination, but the whispers grew louder, and the figures became more defined, revealing a haunting truth hidden beneath the surface of the digital realm.

These whispers were the forgotten and unseen aspects of people's lives, the parts that were often buried beneath carefully curated profiles and glossy images. As Amy delved deeper into the mystery, she realised that behind the façade of picture-perfect posts, there were stories of pain, struggles, and vulnerability waiting to be told.

She discovered that unprincipled producers were creating fake videos, manipulating reality to deceive viewers for profit. Ruthless influencers were driven solely by monetary gain, exploiting their followers' trust to endorse products or services they didn't truly believe in. High-profile cartels were behind the creation of misleading Instagramverse stories, preying on the emotions of unsuspecting users, exploiting tragedies to gain financial advantage.

One of the most egregious campaigns run by the unprincipled producers was a fake video that targeted a sensitive social issue—mental health awareness. They created a heart-wrenching video depicting a young person struggling with depression and contemplating self-harm. The video went viral, tugging at the heartstrings of viewers, who shared it with good intentions to raise awareness about mental health issues.

However, as Amy and the group of good influencers investigated further, they discovered that the video was entirely fabricated. The young person in the video was an actor, and the emotions portrayed were scripted. The unprincipled producers had manipulated reality to deceive viewers into sharing the video, solely to gain profit through ad revenue and sponsorship deals.

Outraged by this deceitful act, Amy and her team decided to launch a counter-campaign. They created an authentic video featuring real individuals who had battled with mental health issues and had overcome their struggles. Each person shared their journey of healing, offering hope and encouragement to others facing similar challenges.

They accompanied the video with a heartfelt message, urging users to be vigilant and discerning about the content they shared. They emphasized the importance of supporting genuine causes and organisations working tirelessly to raise mental health awareness, rather than contributing to the profit-driven agenda of unprincipled producers.

Their campaign gained traction quickly, as users resonated with the message of authenticity and empathy. The genuine video touched the hearts of millions, inspiring a community of support for mental health initiatives. Users began to question the authenticity of viral content before sharing, helping to stem the spread of fake videos and misinformation.

Meanwhile, the ruthless influencers were exploiting their followers' trust to endorse products and services they didn't truly believe in. Amy noticed that many of these influencers would promote diet products, weight loss teas, and supplements, claiming they had used them to achieve their toned physiques.

But behind the scenes, these influencers were following strict diets and undergoing rigorous exercise routines, often with the help of personal trainers and nutritionists. The products they endorsed had little to do with their actual results. Their dishonesty was causing harm, as vulnerable individuals believed that these products were the sole reason for the influencers' appearances, leading to unrealistic expectations and potentially dangerous behaviours.

Amy and her team decided to counter this exploitation by collaborating with genuine fitness experts and nutritionists. They created a series of educational posts and videos, debunking the myths promoted by the ruthless influencers. They encouraged users to prioritize their health and well-being over quick-fix products, promoting sustainable fitness and nutrition practices.

The campaign gained massive support from users who appreciated the honesty and transparency. Many shared their own stories of battling with body image issues and unrealistic beauty standards, finding solace in the message of self-acceptance and genuine wellness.

As for the high-profile cartels behind the creation of misleading Instagramverse stories, Amy and her team uncovered a particularly disturbing scheme. They discovered a profile that claimed to be raising funds for children suffering from life-threatening illnesses, asking for generous donations from users' kind hearts.

However, the truth was far darker. The cartel had fabricated heartbreaking stories about children in need and used emotional manipulation to prey on the empathy of unsuspecting users. They diverted the donations to their own coffers, using the guise of charity to amass illicit wealth.

Amy and the good influencers knew they had to put an end to this exploitation immediately. They reported the profile to Instagramverse, which led to its removal from the platform. They also launched a public awareness campaign, urging users to be cautious and verify the authenticity of charity profiles before donating.

They partnered with legitimate organisations and created a secure donation platform, ensuring that users' contributions went directly to reputable charities supporting children in need. The response was overwhelming, as users showed their unwavering support for genuine causes and united to put an end to such manipulative practices.

Through these campaigns, Amy and her team successfully challenged the unprincipled producers, ruthless influencers, and high-profile cartels that sought to exploit the vulnerability and compassion of Instagramverse users. They transformed the digital realm into a place of authenticity, empathy, and genuine connection, guiding users towards discernment and compassion in their interactions.

As the captivating abyss of Instagramverse continued to evolve, Amy knew that the battle against deception and exploitation was an ongoing one. But armed with the power of truth, empathy, and collective action, she remained committed to protecting the platform from nefarious forces and fostering a community built on genuine connections and positive transformation.

Their united front caught the attention of their followers and sparked a movement within the Instagramverse community. Users began to demand transparency and authenticity from the accounts they followed, seeking real connections rather than empty endorsements. The influence of the deceitful "influencers and cartels started to wane, overshadowed by a wave of empathy and truth.

As Amy continued to hear the whispers of the unseen, she realised that the digital realm of Instagramverse could be a place of healing and closure as well. Inspired by the vulnerability displayed by her fellow users, she decided to create a safe space for people to share their hidden struggles and stories.

Through a series of heartfelt posts and stories, Amy shared her own vulnerabilities and encouraged others to do the same. The response was overwhelming, as users from all walks of life opened up about their battles with mental health, insecurities, and past traumas. The virtual realm became a support network, a place where people could find solace, understanding, and strength in their shared experiences.

As she navigated the whispers of the unseen, Amy discovered the importance of embracing vulnerability, both in herself and in others. The shadowy figures and haunting whispers were not something to be feared but rather a catalyst for growth and healing. The digital realm became a canvas for users to confront their past, embrace their hidden selves, and find solace in their shared humanity.

Amy's journey through the whispers of the unseen transformed her perspective on the power of authenticity and genuine connections. She learned that true strength lay not in hiding behind a facade of perfection but in embracing one's vulnerabilities and using them as steppingstones.

towards growth and healing.

With each whisper, Amy became a source of light, guiding others towards acceptance and self-discovery. She realised that the true beauty of Instagramverse lay in the connections forged through empathy, understanding, and shared experiences. As she continued her adventures, Amy vowed to use her platform to amplify the voices of the unseen and to inspire others to embrace their authentic selves, finding strength in vulnerability and compassion in the forgotten stories that make us human.

CHAPTER 20
"LIFE IN THE REAL WORLD"

Amy felt different. Her life was not filled with hiding away in social media and the Instagramverse world anymore.

By engaging in various activities with her friends and family, participating in charity work, and focusing on her studies, Amy has found a sense of purpose beyond social media. She has grown into a confident and compassionate individual, ready to face the challenges of the real world with the knowledge that true connection and fulfilment lie in living life to the fullest, embracing authenticity, and making a difference in the lives of others.

She decided she was going to become a lawyer so she could deal with online criminality and bring them to justice.

She opened her calendar in her phone and was pleased with herself as she scanned her week ahead.

Day 1: Monday - Study & Charity Work

Amy starts her week by attending her college classes. As she aspires to become a lawyer, she dedicates extra time to her studies, diligently preparing for upcoming exams and working on research projects. In the afternoon, she engages in charity work at a local shelter, helping to distribute meals and essential supplies to those in need.

Day 2: Tuesday - Dance Class & Parents' Chores

On Tuesday evenings, Amy joins a dance class with her friends. Dancing is not only a fun hobby but also a great way to stay active and relieve stress. After the dance class, she returns home and helps her parents with household chores, recognizing the importance of contributing to the family and sharing responsibilities.

Day 3: Wednesday - Hiking Adventure

Midweek, Amy, and her friends plan a hiking adventure in a nearby nature reserve. They immerse themselves in the beauty of nature, enjoying each other's company and appreciating the moments away from screens and devices.

Day 4: Thursday - Lunch with Grandma & Volunteer Work

On Thursdays, Amy takes a break from her college classes and visits her grandmother for lunch. They share stories, laughter, and a special bond that reminds her of the importance of family connections. In the afternoon, she volunteers at a local animal shelter, caring for abandoned.

pets and helping with adoption events.

Day 5: Friday - Movie Night with Friends

As the weekend approaches, Amy and her friends plan a movie night at her place. They gather to watch a selection of classic films and enjoy homemade snacks. The night is filled with laughter and camaraderie, reinforcing the value of offline friendships.

Day 6: Saturday - Beach Cleanup & Coffee with a Mentor

On Saturday morning, Amy participates in a beach cleanup event with an environmental organisation. They collect litter and raise awareness about the importance of protecting marine ecosystems. In the afternoon, she meets with a mentor who is a practicing lawyer, seeking guidance and advice for her future career.

Day 7: Sunday - Family Picnic & Art Workshop

On Sundays, Amy spends quality time with her family. They organize a picnic at a nearby park, playing games and savouring delicious homemade food. In the afternoon, she attends an art workshop, exploring her creative side and expressing herself through various artistic mediums.

As the week comes to an end, Amy reflects on how her life has transformed. She no longer feels the need to hide away in the virtual world of Instagramverse, for she has discovered the richness and fulfilment of real-world experiences and

genuine connections.

Determined to make a positive impact and combat online criminality, Amy continues her journey towards becoming a lawyer. She envisions herself as a force for justice, defending those who have fallen victim to cybercrime and holding perpetrators accountable.

CHAPTER 21:
BREAKING FREE FROM THE SPELL

Amy's journey through Instagramverse's virtual realm, she faced the most perilous challenge yet—a battle to break free from its alluring grasp and protect herself and her loved ones from its dangers. Amy knew that she had to summon all her wisdom, courage, and newfound self-awareness to confront this ultimate test.

Determined to regain control of her life, Amy took a bold step. She got herself another phone and placed her old one in the bottom drawer, cutting off her immediate access to the virtual world. She recognised that breaking free from the spell of Instagramverse required a physical and emotional distance from its tempting allure.

With her mobile phone set aside, Amy stood in her living room, ready to embark on a home workout journey. The space around her transformed into a personal gym, a sanctuary of movement and health. The digital distractions were forgotten, replaced by her determination to stay active and fit.

As the workout video began, Amy's energy surged. Each exercise became a challenge she eagerly embraced, and the mobile phone remained untouched, its allure no match for the thrill of physical activity.

Her body responded to the movements, muscles awakening and embracing the rhythm. Sweat glistened on her forehead, a testament to her dedication and commitment to her well-being.

With each push-up, lunge, and plank, Amy felt her strength and endurance grow. The home workout became more than just a routine; it was a journey of self-discovery, an exploration of her physical capabilities and mental resilience.

As she followed the instructor's guidance, Amy felt a sense of camaraderie with the other participants on the screen. Even though they were physically distant, they were united in the pursuit of health and vitality. The mobile phone sat idly by, but Amy's focus remained unwavering. This was her time to nurture her body and mind, to take a break from the digital realm and fully embrace the present moment.

As the workout came to an end, Amy's heart raced with a sense of accomplishment. She knew that this was just the beginning of her fitness journey, a path she would continue to tread with dedication and passion.

With a smile, she picked up her mobile phone, but the allure of the virtual world had diminished. She had discovered the joy of physical activity, the exhilaration of pushing her limits, and the rewards of staying committed to her health.

Amy made home workouts a regular part of her routine. Her mobile phone became a valuable resource for finding new workout routines and connecting with fitness communities, but she now understood the importance of setting aside time for physical well-being.

In the realm of home workouts, Amy found empowerment and a sense of agency over her health. She discovered that staying active and healthy was not just a physical endeavour; it was a mental and emotional journey of self-care and self-love.

With each workout, she felt her body grow stronger, her mind clearer, and her spirit more resilient. The mobile phone became a tool to enhance her fitness journey, but the true magic lay in the dedication and commitment she brought to her home workouts.

Amy found a new appreciation for her body and its capabilities. She understood that taking care of herself was a gift that extended beyond the digital realm, and in the moments of home workouts, she discovered a wellspring of vitality and happiness.

But just as Amy believed she had taken the necessary precautions; something strange began to happen. The portal to the virtual realm, which had once been closed, seemed to reopen inexplicably. An enigmatic entity, drawn by the portal's allure, started to cross over into Amy's bedroom. The sinister presence cast an eerie shadow, and its intentions remained shrouded in mystery.

At that very moment, Amy's mother entered her bedroom, unaware of the dangerous forces at play. She went about tidying up the room, her eyes falling on the bottom drawer where Amy had stowed away her old phone. Intrigued by her daughter's actions, she opened the drawer to take a closer look.

To her shock and horror, the enigmatic entity reached out and grabbed hold of Amy's mother's wrist with an icy grip. She let out a chilling scream, feeling the presence's malevolence tighten around her. Fear and panic enveloped the room as the entity seemed to feed off the emotions of both mother and daughter.

Amy's instincts kicked in, and she rushed to her mother's side. The entity's presence seemed to grow stronger with each passing second, and Amy knew that she couldn't rely on brute force to free her mother from its grasp. Instead, she drew upon the lessons she had learned throughout her adventures within the virtual realm.

Summoning her courage and empathy, Amy approached the entity with compassion rather than fear. She understood that it thrived on negative emotions and vulnerabilities, much like the malevolent entities she had encountered before. Instead of succumbing to terror, she focused on channelling her inner strength and resilience.

With a determined voice, she addressed the enigmatic entity, speaking directly to its underlying intentions. She acknowledged its presence and expressed understanding of its desire to cross over from the virtual realm. But she also reminded it that its actions were causing harm to her loved ones, and she urged it to reconsider its path.

As the entity seemed to consider Amy's words, hope surged through her veins. It appeared that her approach of compassion and understanding had made an impact. The grip on her mother's wrist loosened slightly, and for a moment, Amy thought they had succeeded in convincing the entity to return to the virtual realm.

But just as quickly as the hope had risen, it was shattered. The entity's hesitation was short-lived, and a malevolent grin crept across its intangible form. It had no intention of going back through the portal. Instead, it had decided that this new world was to its liking, and it was determined to stay.

Amy's heart pounded in her chest as she realised that their situation had become even more perilous. The entity's refusal to return to the virtual realm meant that it intended to wreak havoc in the real world. Panic threatened to overwhelm her, but she knew she had to remain strong for her mother's sake.

With her mother still in the entity's grasp, Amy tugged with all her might, trying to free her from the sinister hold. But the entity's grip was relentless, its presence now fully dislodged from the phone. It seemed to grow stronger as it continued to resist the pull of the portal.

As the struggle intensified, the room filled with an eerie aura. Objects seemed to tremble and shake, and a chilling wind swept through the space. The enigmatic entity had become a force of malevolence, unyielding in its determination to stay in this new world.

Fear coursed through Amy's veins, but she drew upon the courage she had gained from her past encounters. She knew that she couldn't let fear dictate her actions; she had to find a way to protect her mother and herself.

In a moment of clarity, Amy remembered the lessons she had learned about authenticity and empathy. She realised that the entity was drawn to negative emotions and fear. If she could maintain her own sense of calm and show unwavering compassion, it might weaken the entity's hold.

With a deep breath, Amy focused on the love she felt for her mother. She directed all her energy towards the entity, projecting a sense of understanding and empathy. She acknowledged its desire to stay in this world, but she also expressed the pain and harm it was causing.

"I understand that you want to be here, but you're hurting my mother and me," Amy spoke firmly, her voice steady despite the turmoil in her heart. "We need to find a way to coexist peacefully. There must be another path for you."

To her surprise, the entity seemed to waver once more. Its malevolent demeanour softened, and a hint of uncertainty flickered in its ethereal form. Amy continued to hold her ground, not giving in to the fear that threatened to consume her.

As she maintained her compassionate stance, a new realization dawned on her—the entity had once been human too. It was someone lost and trapped in the virtual realm, just like she had been. It had yearned for connection and understanding, but somewhere along the way, it had lost its way and become twisted by its own negative emotions.

With this newfound understanding, Amy felt a surge of empathy for the entity. She could sense its pain and loneliness, and she knew that she had to find a way to help it.

"Let us help you find peace," Amy said gently, reaching out her hand to the entity. "You don't have to be alone in this world. We can find a way for you to coexist with us without causing harm."

The entity seemed to hesitate once more, as if torn between its malevolent nature and the compassion Amy was offering. In that moment, Amy knew that she had planted a seed of hope. She remained patient and understanding, giving the entity the space, it needed to make its decision.

Finally, the entity's form started to waver, and a sense of calm settled over the room. With a soft sigh, it relinquished its grip on Amy's mother's wrist, slowly retreating back towards the portal.

"I will stay, but I will not cause harm," the entity whispered, its voice tinged with sorrow and gratitude. "Thank you for showing me compassion when I had forgotten what it felt like."

As the entity crossed back into the virtual realm, the portal closed once again, sealing it off from the real world. Amy and her mother were left in awe of the experience they had just endured. The encounter had been harrowing, but it had also been a powerful lesson in the transformative power of empathy and understanding.

In the aftermath of their encounter, Amy and her mother decided to keep the portal closed permanently. They recognised the dangers that lurked within the virtual realm and the need to protect themselves and others from malevolent entities seeking to cross over.

As they moved forward, Amy knew that her journey of self-discovery had not truly ended. The allure of the virtual world still beckoned, and new challenges lay ahead. But she felt a newfound sense of strength and wisdom, knowing that she could navigate the digital realm with empathy, compassion, and the resilience she had gained through her experiences.

The final chapter, "Breaking Free from the Spell," had been a test of Amy's courage and understanding. The encounter with the malevolent entity had pushed her to confront the darkness within the virtual realm and discover the transformative power of empathy. As the chapter ended, a sense of anticipation lingered, hinting at the adventures and challenges that awaited Amy in the captivating abyss of Instagramverse.

CHAPTER 22:
AMY'S MOTHER WANTED TO LEARN MORE

In the aftermath of the harrowing encounter with the malevolent entity and the closing of the portal, life settled into a new rhythm for Amy and her family. Amy had found a sense of balance between her digital life and the real world, understanding the importance of authentic connections and being present in the moments that truly mattered.

Reflecting on her Instagramverse odyssey, Amy realised the profound impact it had on her life and those around her. The virtual realm had been a double-edged sword—a place of wonder and excitement, but also one of danger and temptation. Through her journey, she had learned valuable lessons about the dangers of seeking validation from others, the allure of escapism, and the transformative power of empathy and self-discovery.

Amy's relationship with Instagramverse had evolved. She still appreciated the platform for its ability to connect people and share meaningful experiences, but she now used it more mindfully. She focused on being authentic and genuine, sharing her real-life adventures and thoughts without seeking external validation.

As for her relationships in the real world, they flourished. Amy invested time and effort into her family, friendships, and interests, finding fulfilment in the richness of authentic connections. She had come to understand that the digital realm could never replace the depth of human interaction and the joy of shared experiences.

With her mobile phone set aside, Amy sat on the living room floor with her younger brother Danny, surrounded by an array of colourful board games. Laughter filled the air as they excitedly shuffled cards, rolled dice, and set up their game of choice.

Danny's eyes sparkled with delight, eager to engage in a friendly sibling rivalry. The mobile phone sat untouched; its pull diminished by the joy of spending quality time with her brother.

As they began playing, Amy's competitive spirit emerged, but she made sure to strike a balance, offering encouragement and celebrating Danny's victories as much as her own.

With each roll of the dice and move of the game pieces, they engaged in lively banter and friendly teasing. The board games became more than just entertainment; they were a bridge that strengthened the bond between siblings.

The mobile phone remained forgotten, replaced by the warmth of connection and the thrill of shared experiences. Amy knew that this was a moment she wanted to cherish, a memory she would hold dear in her heart.

As the board games continued, the living room filled with camaraderie and joy. Amy and Danny were engrossed in the fun of the games, the hours slipping away without notice.

During their play, they created memories that would last a lifetime—laughs shared, challenges overcome, and the magic of togetherness.

When they finally decided to wrap up their game session, they exchanged high-fives and playful hugs. The mobile phone beckoned, but Amy didn't feel the need to check it immediately. She had experienced something far more valuable—an afternoon of sibling bonding and love.

As she picked up her new mobile phone, she knew that while the digital realm held its allure, the real-world connections with her loved ones were irreplaceable. She made a silent vow to make more time for board games with Danny, recognizing the magic of simple pleasures and quality time spent together.

In the realm of board games, she found a beautiful reminder of the importance of family, the joy of laughter, and the power of being fully present. Each roll of the dice became a symbol of their shared journey, and in the moments spent with Danny, she discovered the priceless treasure of sibling love and camaraderie.

Throughout her journey, Amy's mother had observed her daughter's growth and transformation with pride and awe. She had seen the impact of the digital world on her daughter's life, both positive and negative. Amy's newfound

wisdom and resilience had inspired her, and she couldn't help but be intrigued by the virtual realm that had played such a significant role in her daughter's life.

One day, while Amy was out with her friends, her mother couldn't resist the temptation any longer. She sat in Amy's room, her eyes fixed on the dormant portal that had once connected them to the virtual realm. Curiosity bubbled within her, and she wondered what it would be like to peek inside, just for a moment.

Hesitant yet eager, Amy's mother reached for the phone that had been kept in the bottom drawer. As she held it in her hands, she felt a surge of anticipation and uncertainty. Would she be able to handle what lay beyond the portal? Would she too be drawn into its alluring abyss?

Taking a deep breath, Amy's mother activated the phone and opened Instagramverse. She hesitated for a moment, her finger hovering over the screen. With a mix of excitement and trepidation, she took the plunge, crossing over into the virtual realm.

Inside Instagramverse, Amy's mother was greeted by a whirlwind of captivating images, posts, and stories. The virtual world was indeed enchanting, and she could understand why Amy had been drawn to it. But she also sensed the dangers that lurked beneath the surface—the allure of validation, the risk of losing touch with reality, and the potential for malevolent entities to cross over.

As she explored the digital landscape, Amy's mother kept in mind the lessons her daughter had learned. She embraced empathy and authenticity, connecting with others through meaningful interactions. She marvelled at the power of human connection, even within the confines of a virtual space.

But she also knew that she had to be mindful. The virtual realm was a place of temptation, and she could see how easy it would be to lose oneself in its allure. Recognizing the importance of boundaries, Amy's mother set limits for herself, ensuring that her time on Instagramverse remained balanced with her real-world responsibilities and connections.

When Amy returned home, she found her mother engrossed in the virtual realm. Her face was a mix of fascination and contemplation. As Amy approached her, her mother looked up, a smile playing on her lips.

"I can see why you were drawn to this world," Amy's mother admitted. "It's captivating, but it's also a place where one must be mindful and true to oneself."

Amy nodded, glad that her mother understood the complexities of the virtual realm. She knew that her mother had a newfound appreciation for the impact it could have on people's lives.

From that day on, Amy and her mother navigated the digital world together, supporting each other in staying grounded and true to themselves. They found joy in sharing their real- life experiences, passions, and challenges, strengthening their bond in both the real and virtual realms.

Amy's Instagramverse odyssey had been a journey of self-discovery and growth. It had taught her the value of authenticity, empathy, and human connection. And now, with her mother by her side, Amy felt even more equipped to face the captivating abyss of Instagramverse, knowing that she could strike a balance between her digital life and the richness of the real world.

As the story ended, readers were left with a sense of fulfilment and anticipation. Amy's journey had been one of transformation and resilience, and the impact of her experiences lingered on. With a newfound sense of wisdom and unity, Amy and her mother embraced the unknown adventures that awaited them, both in the captivating digital realm and the profound depths of their real-world connections.

CHAPTER 23:
HIDDEN AGENDA

As Amy sat in the college cafeteria, she overheard a small group of people engaged in a lively discussion about AI technology. It piqued her interest, as she had always been fascinated by the intersection of technology and human experiences. Among the group, she noticed a guy named Wayne, who seemed particularly knowledgeable about the subject.

Intrigued by the conversation, Amy decided to approach.

Wayne during a break between classes. She introduced herself, and they quickly found common ground in their shared interest in technology and AI. They exchanged numbers, planning to meet up after class to continue their discussion.

When the time came for their meeting, Amy felt a sense of excitement and curiosity. She wanted to share her unique experiences with Wayne, including her encounters within the virtual realm of Instagramverse and the existence of the portal. Little did she know that Wayne had a hidden agenda.

As they sat in a quiet corner of the campus, Amy began recounting her incredible journey through the virtual realm. She shared the dangers and allure of Instagramverse, her encounters with malevolent entities, and the transformative power of empathy and self-discovery.

Wayne listened attentively, seeming genuinely interested in Amy's experiences. He asked questions and appeared to be supportive, but behind his affable demeanour lurked ulterior motives. Unknown to Amy, Wayne was the son of one of the

Instagramverse developers, and he had learned about the portal from his father's discussions.

Wayne saw an opportunity to gain access to the virtual realm through Amy's phone. He believed that the portal held immense potential for the company, but he also recognised its dangers. If he could take control of the portal, he could harness its power for his own purposes, all while protecting Instagramverse from the risks it posed.

As the conversation continued, Wayne subtly steered the discussion towards the portal and how it worked. He probed Amy for more details, seemingly fascinated by the idea of such a transformative connection between the real and virtual worlds.

Unaware of Wayne's intentions, Amy excitedly shared the mechanics of the portal, how it had mysteriously opened and allowed her to cross into the virtual realm. She explained that it seemed to have a connection with her emotions, and that she could summon it at will.

Wayne's smile hid a calculating mind. He saw an opportunity to exploit Amy's connection with the portal to further his own goals. He suggested that they meet up again to explore the possibility of experimenting with the portal and its AI elements together. Amy, eager to share her discoveries with someone who seemed genuinely interested, readily agreed.

In the days that followed, Wayne met with his father, the Instagramverse developer, to discuss his findings. He revealed that he had encountered someone who had stumbled upon the portal and had access to the virtual realm. Wayne's father was intrigued but cautious, aware of the risks involved.

Wayne assured his father that he could handle the situation and that he would gain control of the portal without Amy's knowledge.

He believed that he could protect Instagramverse from any potential harm while exploiting the portal's capabilities for the company's benefit.

As Wayne and Amy continued to meet, their friendship grew, and Amy felt a genuine connection with him. Unaware of his true intentions, she remained open and trusting. She shared more about her experiences within the virtual realm, hoping that their shared passion for technology would lead to new discoveries and understanding.

However, as Wayne's plan began to unfold, Amy's instincts started to kick in. She noticed subtle changes in Wayne's behaviour and the questions he asked. Her gut told her that something was amiss, but she couldn't quite put her finger on it.

As Wayne pressed for more information about the portal, Amy's suspicions heightened. She became more cautious about sharing sensitive details and decided to take precautionary measures to protect her phone and the portal. She decided that she was going to put an end to the friendship. She was going to organise a meetup.

Amy hesitated for a moment before picking up her phone to call Wayne. She knew she needed to be cautious, as she dialled his number, her heart raced with apprehension. After a couple of rings, Wayne answered, sounding excited to hear from her. "Hey, Amy! What's up?" he said cheerfully.

"Hey, Wayne," Amy replied, trying to sound casual. "I was wondering if we could meet up tonight. There's something I wanted to talk to you about."

"Sure, I'd love to see you," Wayne said eagerly. "Where do you want to meet?"

"How about the cafe on Maple Street?" Amy suggested. "It's quiet, and we can have some privacy to talk."

"Sounds good," Wayne agreed. "What time should I be there?"

"Let's meet at 7 pm," Amy said, choosing a time that would give her enough space to prepare for the meeting. "See you then."

"Looking forward to it," Wayne replied with a hint of excitement in his voice. "See you at 7."

After ending the call, Amy felt a mix of emotions. Part of her was relieved that Wayne agreed to meet.

As the hours passed, Amy found it challenging to concentrate on anything else. She kept replaying the conversation with Wayne in her mind, trying to pick up on any hints or clues that might reveal his true motives. She knew she had to be careful and guard her phone, even if it meant ending her friendship with Wayne.

Amy's heart pounded in her chest as she heard the creaking floorboard. She knew she was alone in the house, and the sound could only mean one thing - someone was in her room. Fear and suspicion flooded her mind, she had just locked the portal phone away in her dad's safe in the cellar and was already in the kitchen.

Feeling vulnerable and trapped, Amy scanned the room for anything she could use as a weapon. Her eyes fell on a steak tenderising hammer, and she grabbed it tightly, ready to defend herself if needed. Taking a deep breath, she mustered her courage and tiptoed up the stairs towards her bedroom door, trying to stay as quiet as possible.

As she cautiously opened the door, she saw a shadowy figure moving around in her room. Panic gripped her, but she knew she had to confront whoever was invading her space. She stepped forward and flipped the light switch, revealing the intruder's identity.

To her surprise, it was Wayne standing there with an uneasy smile on his face. "Hey, Amy," he said, trying to act nonchalant. "I thought I'd surprise you before our meeting."

Amy's suspicion was confirmed, and her anxiety soared. She knew she couldn't trust Wayne, and his sudden appearance in her room without her consent sent shivers down her spine. "What are you doing here?" she demanded, trying to keep her voice steady.

Wayne looked taken aback by her response but quickly composed himself. "I just wanted to talk to you before our meeting," he replied. "I couldn't wait."

Amy's mind raced with possibilities, wondering if Wayne had somehow heard her coming out of the cellar. She couldn't risk revealing anything to him, so she decided to stick to her plan of ending their association.

"Look, Wayne, I think we need to talk," she said firmly, trying to hide her nerves. "I've been feeling overwhelmed lately, and I need to focus on my studies. I don't think it's a good idea for us to see each other anymore."

Wayne looked disappointed, but he nodded understandingly. "Okay, if that's what you want," he replied, trying to mask his disappointment.

Feeling a mix of relief and concern, Amy ushered Wayne out of her room and closed the door behind him. She knew she had to be cautious and take extra measures to protect the portal and her mobile from prying eyes.

After Wayne left, Amy hurried to the cellar and retrieved her phone from the safe. She knew she couldn't leave the portal unguarded, so she decided to find a more secure hiding place within her room.

With determination, Amy searched her room for a suitable spot, eventually settling on a hidden compartment beneath her bookshelf. She carefully placed her phone inside, making sure it was well-concealed and turned off.

As she locked the hidden compartment, Amy vowed to be more vigilant and cautious in the future. She knew she couldn't trust anyone with the knowledge of the portal, not even someone she thought was a friend.

From that moment on, Amy kept her secret close, ensuring that no one would discover the truth about the Instagram portal. She focused on her studies, her family, and her true friends, cherishing the moments that mattered most in her real-life adventures.

Unbeknown to her the Instagramverse held even more mysteries and challenges that would test her resolve and courage. But armed with her newfound caution and determination, Amy was ready to face whatever came her way, protecting the portal from falling into the wrong hands, and ensuring that the secrets of the Instagramverse remained hers to guard.

Little did Amy know that the stage was set for a thrilling confrontation between her newfound friend and the hidden forces that sought to exploit the power of the virtual realm. As she delved deeper into the world of AI technology and the enigmatic portal, she would soon realise the true depth of the dangers that lurked within the captivating abyss of Instagramverse.

The future held uncertainty, secrets, and the unfolding of a gripping tale that would test Amy's resilience and determination to safeguard the transformative connection between the real and virtual worlds.

She hoped that her phone was truly secure. What she didn't realise was that Wayne had placed a spying devise in her room.

Sucked into the Deception: A review by World Author
September 2024

Diane Shawe, the creative mind behind "Scrolling Shadows," has done it again with her latest young adult novel, "Sucked into the Deception: Amy's Fight to Protect Her Unique Mobile Phone in the Instagramverse." This exciting sequel takes readers on a wild ride through the digital world, building on the themes of technology and self-discovery from the first book.

Amy's New Mission

In this gripping follow-up, we find our hero Amy Richardson facing a whole new challenge. She's now in charge of protecting an incredible mobile phone that can control the digital world and maybe even the entire multiverse. Shawe cleverly raises the stakes, turning Amy's personal struggle with social media addiction into a high-stakes mission that could change everything.

Welcome to the Instagramverse

Shawe's talent for world-building shines as she brings the Instagramverse to life. It is a digital landscape filled with mind-bending puzzles, mysterious security cubes, and sneaky rival hackers, creating a setting that feels like stepping into an immersive video game with real-world stakes.

At the heart of the story is Amy's mission to deliver a powerful phone to the safe haven of Es Vedra.

Her journey is fraught with danger, as she faces shadowy agents from Googleverse, Teslaverse, tiktokverse and more intent on stealing the phone, high-tech drones in relentless pursuit, and rival hackers eager to unlock the phone's secrets. Shawe expertly maintains a fast-paced narrative, with thrilling chases and narrow escapes that keep readers eagerly turning the pages.

A Hero's Evolution. One of the most compelling aspects of the novel is Amy's remarkable character development. Initially overwhelmed, she transforms into a resourceful hero as she navigates the dangers of the Instagramverse.

Support from family and friends provides emotional anchors, while unexpected allies challenge her perceptions and encourage her growth. Among these characters, Wayne stands out with his ambiguous motives, keeping readers guessing about his true allegiance.

As Amy faces each challenge, she not only hones her skills but also discovers her inner strength, making her journey a captivating exploration of self-discovery amidst thrilling adventures.

The story reaches its peak in Es Vedra, a place known for its mystical energy. It's the perfect spot for the final face-off, and Shawe doesn't disappoint with the action-packed scenes. But she also leaves us with some tantalizing hints about what might happen next, making us eager for the next book in the series.

What's Next for Amy?

The book ends with some intriguing questions left unanswered. What other secrets does the phone hold? Will Amy face new challenges in the digital world? And how will her experiences change her in the real world? These open-ended questions have readers eagerly anticipating the next instalments in Amy's journey. "Happening in the Shadow" out soon.

ABOUT THE AUTHOR:

Diane Shawe – Author, Entrepreneur, and Educator

An author with a passion for exploring the intersection of technology, education, and personal growth. Her writing journey began with a love for storytelling and a drive to share knowledge across various fields, from business strategies and personal development to thrilling sci-fi adventures.

With her latest novels 'Scrolling Shadows' and 'Sucked into the Deception', she dives into futuristic landscapes where technology, espionage, and human connection collide. These books are a thrilling journey into the digital realm, following a 17-year-old girl's quest to protect a powerful phone capable of altering reality in the multiverse.

In addition to her fiction works, Diane has authored numerous books aimed at entrepreneurs, business owners, and lifelong learners, including 'The Guide to Guerrilla Growth for Business Owners' and 'The University Goldmine'. These books provide practical insights into personal branding, digital strategy, and business growth in today's competitive environment.

Beyond business, she offer educational guides such as 'Learn How Positive LinkedIn Engagement Can Transform Your Brand', aimed at helping professionals optimise their digital presence. She also write extensively about the hair and beauty industry, drawing from her many years of expertise with titles like 'The Complete Handbook for Braids, Wigs & Hair Care' and 'Getting started in the hair extensions business'.

Each of her current 23 books reflects her commitment to empowering others, whether through thrilling fictional escapades or valuable real-world strategies. Explore her publications and embark on a journey of discovery, learning, and adventure.

Visit Diane Shawe's official Authors Website www.diane-shawe-author.uk

www.ingramcontent.com/pod-product-compliance
Lightning Source LLC
LaVergne TN
LVHW061551070526
838199LV00077B/7002